I0687364

PRINCESS

BOOK 4 OF THE VUKASIN SAGA

B.D. Snowden

GEEKY GOTH PRESS

ISBN: 0-9980843-3-6
ISBN-13: 978-0-9980843-3-6

DEDICATION

This book is dedicated to my daughters and other women who have influenced my life. Strong women. May we see them. May we be them. May we raise them.

ACKNOWLEDGMENTS

Once again this book wouldn't have come together without the wonderful readers of Books, Booze and Betas. I'd like to thank Bebe and Jane. Both of you have no idea how much you have encouraged me when times got tough. I may not have met you in person yet, but you are truly good friends. Thank you.

CHAPTER ONE

Alarms blared and lights flashed as Himeko Tsubaki weaved her way through the rushing warriors. The ship shuddered as it was hit again. This was supposed to have been a simple diplomatic mission, but something had gone wrong.

Himeko had tried to convince the counsel that using the slip-stream technology for travel would be safer while the Tanis remained a threat, especially since they seemed to have developed technology that masked their presence from the Vukasin sensors. But did they listen to her? No. Himeko gave an unlady-like snort as she caught her balance when the ship shifted with another hit. She was so tired of men overlooking her opinion and advice simply because she was a woman. Even her own father dismissed her talents.

Himeko pushed her memories aside. The middle of a crisis situation wasn't the time or place to dwell on the past. After what seemed like forever, Himeko finally made it to the command center of the ship.

"*Kijani,* report!" Himeko shouted over the chaos of the command center.

"Lady Himeko," the surprised commander turned to her, "you really should return to the safety of your quarters." He turned to bark commands at the engineers. "Get those aft shields up before they hit our power cells."

Himeko stared down the *kijani.* "You and I both know that safety anywhere on this ship is an illusion. Now I would rather not have to pull rank, but as the primary diplomat on this ship, I want to know what in the five hells is going on."

"The ship is under attack."

"Obviously," Himeko pursed her lips and crossed her arms across her chest.

"The ship configuration appears to be Polaxian."

"Polaxian?" The pieces started falling into place. The Polaxian species was a mostly humanoid species, that is if humans had been crossbred with big cats. They were a feudalistic society that had a strong reliance on slave labor. Their ruling family had absolute power, and recent intelligence had told the council on Vukas that they had formed an alliance with the rogue Tanis faction. For years the Tanis had been laying the groundwork to take over Vukas and become a ruling power within the interstellar community. Megan and Reijo had thwarted their play for ruling Vukas, but Bel, the leader of the Tanis, still managed to become a major power beyond their planet.

That was how Himeko found herself playing diplomat. Vukas was forced out of their xenophobic policies by the actions of the Tanis, so they were scrambling to form alliances and trade agreements.

The fact that the Polaxians were the ones attacking them meant that somehow the Tanis had found out about the diplomatic negotiations.

"*Kijani*, was the encrypted information about our mission sent to Reijo and Megan?" Himeko demanded.

The commander looked affronted that a

woman would question his reliability. "It was sent as soon as you requested it to be."

Himeko didn't have time to sooth his ego. She was intelligent enough to know that they were severely outnumbered and it was unlikely that they were going to escape. They would be lucky if they made it out with their lives.

"Purge all systems of the information of our mission," Himeko instructed the information officer. The *kija* turned his gaze to his commander, wasting precious seconds. "Now!"

Himeko pulled the journal she kept with her at all times from the satchel she carried. She grabbed a phase gun from a nearby officer's belt. She set it to lethal levels, laid her journal on the deck of the command center and fired. In short order the journal was reduced smoldering ash.

"Do you not think we are capable of protecting you, Lady Himeko?" a voice asked.

"I am unimportant in the big scheme of things. We have to make sure that this information doesn't fall into enemy hands." With that last statement, she turned and ran back to her quarters. Many of the warriors were shocked to see the usually serene and composed Earthling rushing past them.

Himeko had been raised her entire life to know that the individual was meaningless, it was the organization, the family, that mattered. She had lived her life that way with the exception of once when she had railed against the idea of simply being a pretty pawn, somebody's gift in exchange for loyalty or to further her father's organization. The *Tsubaki-kai* was everything, but just once she had wanted her father to be just her dad and not the *kumicho* of a yakuza syndicate. Her anger at the organization coming before his own daughter had sent her seeking solace in the quiet temple on the outskirts of Tokyo.

While part of her regretted her actions, Himeko recognized the hand of fate. She wouldn't go back even if she could because her presence would bring dishonor to the *Tsubaki-kai* and in turn her father. If she was honest with herself, she wouldn't go back because she felt like she had found her place in the universe here. She had built her own family who trusted her skills and knowledge. Here her opinion mattered, even if she had to remind the men from time to time of that fact. She was helping to create a world where females weren't just relegated to roles of pretty accessories. Her work mattered and she would not dishonor those that believed in her even if she were to die today.

Himeko burst through the door of her quarters.

"Ship security lock, command code alpha six eight nine delta." The ship acknowledged her command and she heard the click of the lock engaging.

She accessed the computer systems to make sure that the information officer had followed her instructions. She then set about purging all the information she had encrypted for only her and Megan to see. Thankfully, she had sent that information off days ago, so Megan should be able to continue the negotiations.

Himeko was in the middle of destroying all hard copies (she still preferred handwritten notes) when she was thrown to the floor as the entire ship rocked.

"Hull breach section 46-D, level three," a computerized voice repeated over and over again.

Himeko knew that the breach was near her quarters. She hurried to finish disposing of the sensitive information. Himeko was pulling out the last of her notes when the door to her quarters was wrenched open. The twisted mass of metal was thrown aside and three huge aliens entered, filling her space.

She thought she had become accustomed to being around individuals that dwarfed her, but the Polaxians were massive. They weren't much taller than the typical Vukasin, but they were more heavily muscled and their predatory appearance made them even more menacing.

The lead alien scented the air and spotted the smoldering pile of papers. He snarled and growled something to the other two. Himeko knew from experience that it would take a little while for the translator implanted in her brain stem to catch up with the new language.

The other two aliens turned and left the room. The remaining advanced on Himeko until she could feel its hot breath on her face. She knew he was trying to intimidate her. Inwardly it was working, but she refused to show that outwardly.

She didn't move an inch. She sanely clasped her hands in front of her and stood facing ahead. She stood like a beautiful statue as the Polaxian growled at her.

Slowly the growls turned into a language she could understand. The Polaxian was demanding the location of the diplomat aboard this vessel. The only sign of Himeko's annoyance was the clenching of her jaw. It seemed even in the vastness of the universe that men had difficulty with the idea of a woman being in a position of power. Part of Himeko wanted to shout at the male in front of her that she was the diplomat, but she remained silent. Now was not the time to lose her temper.

One of the others returned to inform the male Himeko assumed was the leader that the crew in the command center was now dead. Himeko closed her eyes and willed away the tears that threatened. In her time aboard this ship she had come to know that the crew were honorable men and their deaths were just a waste.

"Pack the rest away into the holding cells," the Polaxian leader informed his men. "They will fetch a good price on the slave block."

"What about the female?"

The leader turned his gaze on Himeko, "I will take her. I have a feeling she has secrets I have yet to discover."

The leader reached for the silent Himeko. Years of study in various dojos run by the *Tsubaki-kai* and daily katas had her reacting instinctively. She flipped the massive male using his own momentum against her. Only Megan, who had become her sparring partner before Megan's pregnancy, knew the extent of Himeko's training. The rest just viewed her as the serene, delicate beauty of the council.

The male stayed on the floor with a look of shock on his face. It wasn't until his subordinate chuckled that he reacted. He jumped up to face Himeko, who had used his shock to move into a fighting stance. With two large opponents in such a confined area, Himeko was at a disadvantage. Her eyes darted around her quarters. She had to find a way past these men. If she could get out of the room she might have a chance.

When the leader attacked, she leapt on the table near her and launched herself over him. She hit the shoulder of the second Polaxian, using him as a stepping stone to get to the door. Unfortunately, once she passed the threshold of the door, she realized that she had made a grave miscalculation.

She had forgotten about the third Polaxian that had originally been in her quarters. He had been outside of her door standing guard. He easily grabbed her as she ran through the door of her quarters. He pinned her arms and lifted her into the air. She had no purchase to get leverage against him. Without leverage, she had no hope of defeating an enemy twice her size. But she refused to submit.

The leader exited her quarters and snatched her from his subordinate.

"You are going to regret that, little female." Himeko could feel spittle splash against her face. She put her mask in place and refused to react. Her composure just seemed to enrage her capture. He shoved her back into the arms of the other Polaxian. "Take her and confine her separately from the others."

"Is she not going up for auction?"

The leader struck the Polaxian that dared question him. Himeko wanted to wince as she heard the breaking of bones, but she kept her mask in place. To the credit of the injured Polaxian, he didn't cry out in pain. He just held his bleeding nose, crossed his arm across his chest and bowed.

"I apologize for my insolence, my lord."

The Polaxian holding her placed a device on

her back. When he activated it, she felt as if she had been cocooned in ropes from neck to ankle, but she couldn't see any bindings. She shifted, testing her bonds. Himeko gasped as she was squeezed tighter.

"If you value your life, little female, I would refrain from struggling," the leader turned towards her with a sneer. "Those energy bands will crush you if you become unruly." He chuckled as if the idea of her death was a joke.

She was picked up and slung over the shoulder of the Polaxian that bound her. She hoped that Megan would recognize the message she had sent out before her capture. It was a gamble that the other Earthling would recognize the Morse code embedded in the static of the audio message. But Himeko wanted the Polaxian to dismiss the message if it was intercepted and that was the only thing she could think of in the heat of the moment.

CHAPTER TWO

"What do you mean Himeko is missing?" Daray bellowed as he burst through the council chamber door.

Reijo looked up startled. The Nardo clan leader was normally a very calm and composed man. He cringed when his yelling woke the sleeping babe in Megan's arms. Their son had been born just a few weeks ago. With the women from Earth and some found on Ludus Prime, the joys and trials of children were once more filling Vukasin households. There was still a great disparity in numbers between the genders, but for once the men of Vukas had hope again.

Megan eyed Reijo expectantly. He had asked

her to see him so he could break the news to her himself. Himeko was her "BFF." Reijo wasn't sure what that meant exactly, but it evidently held great significance to the women of Earth.

He watched his beloved mate as she soothed their son. It amazed Reijo to learn of a mother's love through the women of Earth. Even many of the Vukasin mothers had tracked down their offspring once it was made clear that they had the right as their mothers to know their children. Vukas was slowly returning to a society that valued the bonds of family once more.

Megan cleared her throat and pointedly looked at Reijo, then at Daray. Reijo sighed. This was the part of being *kijani-a* he hated most. He had already spent the morning notifying the clans of the loss of their sons. Now he had to shoulder the burden of his mate's grief as well as his friend's.

"Sit down, Daray." Reijo motioned to a seat across from him.

The Nardo leader sat, his hands clenched on the table. It still surprised him to see the man so agitated. Reijo knew that Daray took his responsibilities seriously, but he had lost people he was responsible for in battle and Daray had always received the news with quiet composure. The man before Reijo was acting out of character and Reijo wasn't sure why.

"As you know, Himeko and a contingent of warriors went on a diplomatic mission to the Kassis home world."

"Did those twice damn lizards do something to Himeko?" Daray interrupted Reijo.

Megan reached over and laid a hand on Daray's clenched fist. "Put your prejudices aside and listen to the entire account, please."

Daray ducked his head and sighed. "I'm sorry, Lady Megan." He took a deep breath and looked up at Reijo. "I beg your pardon, *Kijani-a*. Please continue."

Reijo nodded his thanks to Megan. "As I was saying, they had a diplomatic mission to Kassis—a mission that was a success. Himeko was able to negotiate not only a fair trade agreement but a treaty that makes the ruling house of Vukas allies with the ruling house of Kassis. Their king was impressed that Zamira, and by extension Ghaleb, would champion the rights of the Kassians created by the Tanis experiments. While having a reputation for

14

being brutal, the Kassian royal family does have a strong sense of honor."

"If the mission was a success, then what happened to Himeko?" Daray asked.

"We don't know for certain. We received a garbled audio message from the *Victory*. When asked to resend the message, we received no response. Since the last known location was near Kassisian space, we asked them to investigate. They found the remains of the disabled ship. It had obviously been attacked. They guarded the vessel until we were able to dispatch our own people to investigate."

"If Himeko is listed as missing, then I assume you haven't found a body yet." Megan rocked her now sleeping son as she quietly asked Reijo questions.

"We only found the bodies of the bridge crew and the odd warrior in the rest of the ship. The majority of the crew is unaccounted for." Reijo ran a hand through his hair, tugging at it in frustration. "You have to understand that there were several hull breaches. It is very likely that the missing crew was sucked into the vacuum of space and are dead."

"Himeko is alive. I would feel it here," Daray thumped his chest with his fist, "if she no longer lived."

Megan gave Reijo an 'I told you so' look. She had insisted that Himeko and Daray had feelings for each other, but Reijo argued that they didn't since it had been a couple of years now and their relationship had not progressed beyond friendship. Megan had argued that they just moved at their own pace. Seeing Daray's distress and conviction Reijo had to concede that Daray at the very least viewed Himeko with something much stronger than the bonds of friendship.

"What about the audio message you mentioned?" Megan asked. "Has anyone tried to clear it up?"

"All the techs could get out of it were a series of blips. They are assuming that sending it was an error or the person sending it was killed before they could speak." Reijo sighed, "It is useless to us."

"I want to hear it anyway," Megan said as she shifted their son to her shoulder and patted his back when he started to stir.

"I don't see what good it would do, my love,"

Reijo said. "While you have many talents, technology isn't one of them."

"You are never going to let me live down the fact that I caused your holoprojector to explode are you?" Megan gave a brief smile at the shared memory before becoming sober once more. "I still want to hear it, Reijo...please."

"Fine." Reijo punched a sequence of keys on the crystal display in the middle of the council table. Soon the room was filled with static white noise, but there was something under the white noise.

"Is this the cleaned up version?" Megan asked.

"No that was the original message," Reijo responded.

"Can I hear what the techs found when they cleared out the static?"

Reijo pushed a few more keys.

Beep, beep, beep, beeeeeeep, beeeeeeep, beeeeeeep, beep, beep, beep

That pattern was repeated twice more before a different pattern began.

"Play the beginning again." Megan stared intently at Reijo.

He played it again.

"Dot, dot, dot, dash, dash, dash, dot, dot, dot." Megan shook her head and smiled. "This wasn't a mistake. Those beeps are your message."

Daray whipped his head around to look at Megan. "What do you mean?"

"Only someone from Earth would have recognized this as a message. That first pattern of three short sounds, three long, with three short again is Morse code for S.O.S."

"What is Es Oh Es?" Reijo inquired.

"In the English alphabet it was the abbreviation for 'save our ship.' It ultimately because a universal signal for distress and asking for help," Megan explained.

"What about the rest of the message?" Daray demanded.

"I'm sorry. I am not familiar enough with Morse code to be able to tell you that."

Daray slumped in his chair.

"But, the information Ghaleb downloaded from Earth might have the rest of the Morse code alphabet, unless it was secret information." Reijo turned questioning eyes to Megan.

"No, anyone with internet access could find the code. It wasn't a secret. But it was set up with the English alphabet, so I would suggest we write down the pattern...dots for short sounds, dashes for long sounds...then I will use the code to spell out the message."

Reijo nodded to Megan and called the techs to start looking for the information she suggested. He informed Megan and Daray it would take a couple of hours since they hadn't catalogued more than a fraction of the downloaded information from Earth.

"If that is the case, I am going to go feed our son and hand him over to a caretaker for a little while. I will return after he is settled." Megan got up, and the men scrambled to stand as she exited the room with the baby.

Reijo returned to his seat, but Daray remained standing.

"Can I speak to you as my friend and not as *kijani-a* of the Imperial army?" Daray asked.

"Of course."

"Is Ghaleb going to look for Himeko and the others?"

Reijo sighed and leaned back in his chair. Daray took it as a bad sign.

Reijo looked over at Daray, "I'm not going to lie to you, Daray. I don't know how much in the way of resources Ghaleb can dedicate to a search that may prove fruitless. We are preparing for open war with the Tanis and playing catch up when it comes to finding allies. Not to mention the Tanis have still managed to use guerilla tactics to keep unrest going here on Vukas."

Daray gave a wary quirk to his lips, "I kind of figured as much." He sat down and looked intently at Reijo. "The Nardo have taken to Himeko much like the Tiaret did with Megan. Did you know that Himeko's name means 'princess' in her culture? That's how the Nardo refer to Himeko…she is The Nardo Princess."

"Where are you going with this, Daray?"

"The Nardo are not going to give Himeko up as long as there is hope."

"The Nardo or you?"

"Does it matter?"

Reijo gave a slight chuckle, "I suppose not."

"If it were Megan missing, what would you do?"

"I would tear the universe apart to find her," Reijo growled.

*****

A few hours later the trio had gathered once more. They had transcribed the blips and beeps into dots and dashes. The techs had been able to find a visual of the Morse code alphabet. Now it was up to Megan to figure out the message Himeko was trying to send.

"P…O…L…A…X." Megan looked over the entire message. Himeko sent a distress call with just this one word. "Polax…that is the message Himeko was trying to send."

Reijo cursed and Megan knew why. Their

intelligence network had recently confirmed that the Tanis had formed an alliance with the Polaxian home world.

"You know what this probably means, right?" Daray asked.

"Our missing people are probably being sold as slave labor," Reijo growled. After rescuing a group of people from one of the Tanis mining slave camps, Reijo had a particular disgust for slavery. Seeing the conditions that slaves had to survive had angered him beyond belief. He had almost singlehandedly freed every slave on Vukas and convinced Ghaleb that they shouldn't trade or ally themselves with worlds who condone slavery. Because Vukas was one of the most technologically advanced races in the galaxy, that decision had pushed other worlds to crack down on the illegal slave trade.

"Will Ghaleb be willing to put resources towards a search now?" Daray inquired.

Megan put a small hand on Reijo's arm and gave a squeeze. "I know how you feel, my love, but don't make commitments for Ghaleb that he may not be able to keep."

"How can you…" Megan laid a finger across Reijo's lips to silence his rant.

"The idea that those I love and care about are in the bonds of slavery tears me up inside. But Ghaleb has to balance the well-being of an entire race as well as our allies when making a decision."

"They attacked a diplomatic vessel. That is an act of war," Daray growled.

Megan turned towards the Nardo clan leader. "And we may yet find ourselves at war."

"So we should just sit here and do nothing?" Daray demanded.

"I didn't say that either," Megan said.

"Then what do you suggest?" Reijo asked. He had long ago learned that his wife was quite savvy when it came to maneuvering the political landscape.

"We need to inform Ghaleb of this new development. Let him and I work the political angle of this. Unfortunately, we all know that political wheels turn slowly. In the meantime," Megan smiled a vicious smile, "We rulers have no control over what a private citizen chooses to do."

Megan stood and left the room to discuss things with Ghaleb. Reijo rose to follow her.

Before exiting the council chamber, he turned to Daray. "I believe the construction on *The Revenge* is completed. It is our most advanced warship to date. It is still docked at the shipyard on Nardo's coast isn't it?"

Reijo didn't wait for Daray to answer before he exited the room.

CHAPTER THREE

Himeko sat at the low table of the Polaxian leader. She had since discovered that he was the youngest son of the royal family and called Listar. He was an ambitious male in a culture that seemed to use assassination and subterfuge as a means for advancement.

Himeko had known that something important was to happen that night because Listar shoved a Polaxian clothing replication unit at her and instructed her to create formal attire for the evening. The Polaxians had created the technology after one too many important people were assassinated by their tailors and seamstresses. Really, what did they expect when their entire workforce was brutalized slaves? Polax wasn't a culture of benevolent servitude; even the highest slave was beaten on a regular basis. Himeko sported her share of bruises from their treatment, though not as much as others because Listar became bored at her stoic reactions.

Himeko took the unit and programmed traditional Japanese attire. While she created a beautiful phoenix design into the kimono, she opted out of the formal kimono for ease of movement. She didn't want to trip on the excess fabric. The replication unit was also able to create accessories. If Listar had remained long enough to see the smile that spread across Himeko's face he would have known he made a tactical error.

Himeko programmed the unit to create a *tessen*, a Japanese war fan. At first glance it seemed like an elegant accessory, but it was made in such a way that the spines could prove lethal. In trained hands, it was as deadly as a sword, and Himeko's father had her trained in *tessenjustu* since she was a child. The life of a yakuza was a dangerous one, after all.

Himeko dressed for the evening. She had created a deep red kimono with intricately painted phoenixes along the hem and sleeves. She patterned them after the masterpiece of a tattoo that adorned her back. That tattoo had been her distinction within the *Tsubaki-kai*. Her father hadn't allowed her the full-body tattoos that the other members of the organization carried, even though she had become their greatest lawyer and no one could defeat her in combat when she carried the *tessen*. Saving her father's life with her skills hadn't been enough to be fully acknowledged as a member of the organization simply because she was a woman—a woman her father decided to sell off in marriage to form an alliance with another organization.

Himeko shook the memories from her head. She centered her mind as the familiar task of tying an obi and ensuring elegant lines in her kimono cleared her mind. She carefully dressed her hair, adding sharp jeweled pins that could be used as a weapon if necessary. Lastly, she tucked her war fan into her obi.

With her preparations complete, she sat in perfect posture in the center of the room used to confine her.

Listar threw open the door and Himeko didn't flinch. She remained still as a china doll, her hands gracefully folded in her lap. Listar was both drawn to her cold beauty and frustrated by his inability to crack her calm exterior.

He prowled around her as she sat quiet and still. The costume was very different from the clothing he had captured her in. It looked both simple and complicated at the same time. There was a regal elegance to the styled hair adorned with jewels. Her face was pale as if she had lightened it, but she had painted her lips a deep red to match the material of her attire and her eyes were emphasized with a touch of color. To Listar she looked almost mythical.

"What is that creature on your gown?" Listar demanded, pointing to the golden phoenix painted on her sleeves.

"Suzaku, the guardian deity of the south. A symbol of the imperial empress of Japan and the *mon* of the *Tsubaki-kai*." Himeko delivered this explanation in the soft spoken voice of a traditional Japanese woman.

Listar just stared at her. He hadn't honestly believed she would answer him as she hadn't spoken a word the entire time he held her captive. He marveled how such a delicate-looking creature was able to give off such a presence of strength. She never attacked. He hadn't seen her draw blood. But his intuition still told him that she was probably stronger than any warrior he had met. He was beginning to understand why the Tanis had wanted her dead. But she was his capture—his prize. That made her his to do with as he pleased, and he still wanted to unwrap her mysteries.

He wanted to press her for more details, but the chimes echoed through his palace announcing that his guests had arrived. So instead he placed the golden collar and chain of slavery upon her neck.

He tugged on the chain, "Come. Dinner is about to be served."

Himeko gracefully rose from her seated position on the ground. Standing just increased her regal appearance. Listar paused to admire the effect she created. It was as if he were leading a beautiful work of art instead of a woman held in slavery against her will. If she had been Polaxian, he would have claimed her as his bride because none had ever captured his attention in the way she had.

He shook his mane and snarled until his sharp canines appeared. She wasn't Polaxian. No matter what strange spell she wove, she was beneath him—simply a slave.

He turned and walked out of her prison, leaving her to follow behind.

*****

Himeko shouldn't have been surprised to see Bel of the traitorous Tanis seated at Listar's dinner table. Bel would want to use the youngest son's ambition to further his own agenda. But she still had not expected to see the man responsible for her kidnapping from Earth. This caused her to stop moving forward until Listar tugged on the chain attached to the collar around her neck.

Himeko took a deep breath and dropped her serene mask firmly in place. She fell back onto old etiquette training, which proved surprisingly easy as Polaxian furniture and customs were quite similar to those of Earth's Asian cultures. They dined seated on cushions around low tables, much like Japan or China. Slaves brought the courses and kept the guests supplied with drink.

Himeko sank to her knees next to Listar. She folded her hands in her lap and stared straight ahead.

"I heard you had attacked a Vukasin vessel, Listar," Bel stated between drinks. "Why is the breeder known as Himeko still alive?" He slammed his goblet on the table, spilling its contents. Before the liquid even settled, a slave scurried over to clean the mess and refill Bel's cup.

Listar calmly placed his goblet on the table. The hackles of his mane rising in his irritation. "My battle, my prize. I will do with this Himeko as I please."

"Sell her to me," Bel demanded.

"No."

That simple statement from Listar had Bel turning purple. The Tanis leader had probably assumed he was the power in this room since he was dealing with a youngest son. But Listar was still Polaxian, and a royal at that. This was his palace and in this small sphere at least, he was the authority.

Listar was shrewd enough to know that his refusal to relinquish Himeko placed his plans in jeopardy. After all, if he was to wrest power from his brothers, he needed the Tanis dog.

Listar took a drink of wine and then used his fingers to pick up a savory morsel of meat from his plate. He chewed thoughtfully while Bel fumed. "I wish to keep her a while longer, but I might be persuaded to allow you to use her for the night."

Himeko removed her fan from her obi and opened it. Anyone watching would see a woman cooling herself or perhaps acting coy behind the painted fan. Only she knew that she was preparing for battle. She knew that due to Polaxian concerns, every person was scanned for energy weapons before entering the private residences. No one came unarmed, of course, but they were reduced to old fashioned blades, many of which were mostly decorative, though the warriors kept a lethal edge on theirs.

Even Bel had a ceremonial sword at his side with a secondary knife on his belt. But Himeko had seen enough of Bel's corpulent figure back on Tanis when she was first taken from Earth to know the man rarely trained as a warrior. He expected his underlings to do the dirty work while he sat back in safety.

If Listar actually handed her over, she was going to kill Bel. She knew that would most likely mean her death, but taking out Bel would go a long way towards keeping the Vukasins from all-out war—a noble sacrifice. Her only regret would be not telling Daray how much he had come to mean to her. She treasured his quiet strength and compassion. She prayed that one day he would find a female deserving of him.

Himeko watched Bel. She could see him calculating in his mind. She knew that he fully planned on killing her, even if Listar demanded she survive the night. To Bel, her death was more important than the demands of a fifth son. He could always move on to one of the other equally ambitious siblings to keep his plans moving forward. But everyone on Vukas, and by extension Bel, knew that Himeko was very dear to Megan. They were the best of friends and confidants. Bel wanted Himeko dead because he could not reach the woman who acquired the Spear of Authority, and therefore the right to rule the Vukasin Empire should she choose to. It didn't matter to Bel that Megan hadn't exercised that right and Ivalio still held the throne. It only mattered that Megan had snatched the power Bel had planned and manipulated towards for years from his hands.

Bel and Listar finished discussing their arrangements for her transfer for the night. When Listar handed Bel her chain, Bel roughly pulled her close. Himeko snapped her *tessen* shut, and with a single sharp thrust, she stabbed Bel between the ribs.

Almost immediately, Listar's and Bel's guards fell on her. She was able to trade blows with the first wave, but soon she was overpowered by sheer numbers because she was out of weapons. Her war fan still protruded from the wheezing Bel. She was fairly certain she had punctured his lung, but she hadn't been able to thrust the fan far enough through his fat to hit his heart. Her hair pins were lost in the guards. When she was reduced strictly to hand to hand combat, it didn't take long for them to pin her to the ground.

Listar stood over her, clapping with an evil smirk on his face. "Finally broke through your icy exterior to discover a volcano of fire beneath." He looked over at the injured Bel and waved his men to take the man away for treatment. He might personally think that the fat and lazy Tanis deserved to die, but he still needed him, unfortunately.

Himeko glared at Listar. She was disheveled, no longer the perfectly composed doll, and she was angry. All of the fear, anger, and resentment she had buried beneath her mask came spilling forth.

"I want to see more of that beautiful fire," Listar exclaimed. "I think I have the perfect place for you, little bird."

CHAPTER FOUR

"Daray, you better bring that *frexing* ship back right now!"

The communications officer had to adjust the volume down before the *Khalon* burst their eardrums. Daray had been ignoring his messages until they were far enough from Vukas' orbit to make it difficult for the military to retrieve them.

He had finally answered because Ghaleb was not just his ruler but his friend and he owed him an explanation.

"Ghaleb, if you would just calm down," Daray started.

"Calm down!" Ghaleb banged so hard on the table in front of him that his holoimage shook. "I expect Banji and Akia to pull this kind of stunt, but not you. I thought you were more level-headed than that."

"I'm bringing her home," Daray simple stated.

"By the twin moons." Ghaleb's holoimage wiped a hand down his face. "What kind of spell are these Earth women able to weave."

"I love her." Daray swept his hand around to indicate the ship's crew. "We all love her." Murmurs of assent bubbled up from the rest of the crew.

"Stealing that ship is an act of treason," Ghaleb growled.

"Then arrest me when I return. I will come peacefully once I know Himeko is safe." Daray held Ghaleb's gaze until the man sighed.

"You know Megan and I are pursuing every political lead to find her and the others."

"I have to do this, Ghaleb. For the last couple of years I stood aside and never took action. I can't do it again." Daray squared his shoulders and faced down the ruler of Vukas. "I won't do it again."

"You understand that I can't openly condone you taking a warship into sovereign territory. You and your crew will be on your own."

Daray looked around the command center. Each man nodded and gave a salute to their leader. Daray knew that each and every one had volunteered for this assignment even after it was explained that they would be stealing the warship. They all wanted to find the woman they considered the princess of the Nardo.

Daray turned back to Ghaleb. "We understand."

"Fine. As far as the rest of the galaxy is concerned, I was unable to contact you. You are now officially rogue."

"And when we get home?" Daray asked.

"We'll discuss that after." Ghaleb reached to turn off communications.

"I only ask that you punish me and not my men. They were just following orders."

Ghaleb didn't respond before cutting off the communicator.

"Sir," an officer said.

"What is it, Arash?" Daray turned to his second in command.

"I have found some chatter about an upcoming slave auction on a moon on the outskirts of the Polaxian territory."

"Change course. We have some merchandise to look over." Daray turned to leave the command center. He trusted his men to handle the flight of the ship. Ghaleb may have to distance himself from what the Nardo men were doing, but Daray still had friends in high places.

His primary goal was to get the woman he loved back, but he couldn't in good conscience leave any Vukasins in the hands of slavers. *The Revenge* was one of the most technologically advanced ships in the known galaxy. With his skilled crew it was possible that they could hit the slave auction with guns a blazing and get out. That scenario was reckless though and Daray wasn't a reckless man.

He unbuttoned his uniform as he walked into his quarters. He pulled up an encrypted communication line.

"About time you contacted us." Megan's fiery hair filled the holoimage until she backed up enough for Daray to see her. "You know Ghaleb is stomping around the palace shouting about the perils of Earth women," Megan said with a slight giggle.

"I'm assuming you have come up with some sort of plan?" Reijo entered the image, wrapping an arm around his mate's shoulder. He leaned in to place a gentle kiss on her forehead, and Daray felt a pang of jealousy in his chest thinking that could be him and Himeko.

"We have information about a slave auction just outside of Polaxian territory." Daray poured himself rajia tea to fight off his exhaustion. After taking a healthy gulp, he continued, "It if fairly safe to assume that if they did take any of the crew to be sold that at least some of them would be there."

Reijo frowned. "A lot of ships from some of the most brutal cultures will be there are well."

"Which is why he is contacting us. Isn't it, Daray?" Megan supplied.

Daray inclined his head, "As much as I am loath to give money to such an enterprise, the prudent thing to do would be buy our people back if there are any there. Otherwise it would be a bloodbath."

"Ghaleb is going to kill me," Reijo sighed.

"Maim you maybe, not kill you," Megan smiled up at her husband. "He doesn't want to have to handle all of the military stuff on top of all of the political stuff."

Reijo shook his head, but he smiled. Daray envied their easy comradery. They always seemed to fit together, even early on in their relationship. Daray thought of Himeko. He adored her, but in the back of his mind he always had this thought that perhaps he wasn't good enough for her. His clan had started calling her the Nardo Princess because they found out that her name meant 'princess' back on Earth. But Daray had thought of her like royalty while he felt like a peasant in her presence. He couldn't blame her for his feelings. Himeko had never treated him with anything but kindness and respect, even when she stood up to him in the beginning. Along the way, they had developed a comfortable habit between them, even if it seemed like they would never be more than friends or colleagues.

"Daray?"

Daray looked up to see Reijo and Megan staring at him. He realized that they had been trying to get his attention while he was lost in thought.

"Sorry. What did you say?"

Reijo looked like he wanted to say something to Daray, but shook his head and responded, "I said that I am going to have Ghaleb allocate credits to build a replacement for *The Revenge*. That should be enough to get most if not all of the missing crew back. But it also means you have to bring that twice-damned ship back in one piece."

"How are you going to get the credits to me?" Daray asked. "We will be at the auction site within two days."

"I'll get Kavi in on that. The old buzzard-raptor has been complaining that he doesn't have enough to do lately." Reijo turned to send a message to the spy master.

"Have him pull on some of his contacts to see if we can pinpoint where Himeko is, especially if she isn't at this auction."

"All right. Look for further communication

in the near future. If someone other than myself or Kavi contacts you, look for the code word 'princess' in the communication. Otherwise it isn't from us."

"Understood."

"Daray, good luck," Megan said before they switched off the holoimage.

Daray stared at the place where the holoimage had projected for a few moments. He hoped that he was doing the right thing. If it had just been him, he wouldn't have any doubts. But this ship was huge and required a full crew to operate, so he was dragging others into what may turn out to be a futile effort. Even if they succeed, they may still face charges of treason when they returned to Vukas. Was it fair to possibly destroy so many lives for a single woman?

Daray wasn't sure he could answer that objectively. While the clan leader in his mind pushed questions through his mind, his heart firmly stood its ground declaring that nothing was more important than Himeko. Without her, nothing else in life mattered.

It kind of scared him that after decades of being a rational man ruled by reason to discover that even he could be swept away by emotion. It was an uncomfortable feeling, but he couldn't bring himself to regret it.

Daray had been going through life fulfilling his duty but not really living. He hadn't really felt fear or desire until Himeko came into his life. She brought him to life. Unfortunately he had never told her how important she was to him.

She had been placed in their stronghold by the sea and quickly became the thread that connected the clan together. She just fit. It wasn't the explosive passion of the others. It was quieter than that.

Daray flopped down on his bunk. Did the fact that his emotions for Himeko crept up on him slowly until she was such a part of him that he couldn't imagine her not being there mean they weren't as powerful as the outwardly passionate emotions of people like Reijo and Megan?

No, they were there even in their quiet existence. He may not be as showy in his feelings for Himeko as Reijo was with Megan, but his connection to Himeko was just as deep. She was the reason he woke in the morning. It was for the sake of Himeko and the future he hoped they could have together that he labored to secure the fortunes of the Nardo. He would go to the ends of the galaxy to ensure her safety and happiness. Five hells, he stole an imperial war ship to find her.

Daray shook his head at himself. He was a fool for even questioning whether he loved her as much as Reijo loved Megan. He was learning that love didn't have to be showy to be strong. Love was as different as the people who experienced it.

He rolled over on his bunk to try and get some rest. His mind played memories of the last time he saw Himeko over and over again. He lifted a prayer to the twin moons that she was safe. He had no idea what he would do in a world that didn't contain Himeko in it.

The ship communicator buzzed just as he was drifting off into sleep. Daray heaved a sigh. No sleep for him again tonight evidently. He rolled over and stared at the ceiling while the comm buzzed again.

"Daray," he answered.

"My lord, we have a Kassian ship to our starboard. Their hail claims they have urgent business with Daray of Nardo." The voice on the other end of the communication paused. "How do you want us to handle this?"

Daray rolled into a sitting position and then stood. He looked down at his wrinkled uniform and straightened it as best he could. While he loathed to appear before an alien species in a disheveled state, he just didn't have the energy to change right now. Once he dealt with the Kassians, he would tell his crew not to disturb him unless the ship was on fire for a few hours.

"I will be on the bridge shortly. Ask them to wait for a moment."

"Understood, my lord."

Daray ran a hand through his hair. He almost walked out without running a comb through it to make it presentable, but old habits are almost impossible to break. He took one last look at his image and decided he was presentable enough before walking out of his quarters to head to the command center.

CHAPTER FIVE

Himeko opened and closed the *tessen* that
Listar had returned to her. She was disappointed to
learn that she had failed to kill Bel of Tanis. She
knew from his quick departure from the area that she
at least had rattled his cage. She also paid close
attention to what the others slaves were saying about
Bel. It would appear that the Tanis resources were
much more extensive than any of them had assumed.
The traitorous clan had secretly created a trading
empire outside of the Vukasin home world. They
actually had no need for Vukas any longer. It
seemed that conquering their native planet was
simply a matter of vanity, the culmination of
generations of grudges against the Ivalio. It was
stupid testosterone-filled posturing.

What worried Himeko was the fact that Bel had informed Listar of exactly who she was. The Polaxian was completely unconcerned that the elite of Vukas would come looking for her. He dismissed the Vukasins as an annoyance and nothing more, despite being one of the most technologically advanced species in the known galaxy. That told her the xenophobic policies of the past few generations had truly isolated Vukas, turning what should have been a superpower into a joke. If she ever made it back, Himeko was going to push the need for more diplomacy.

Make it back? Himeko looked around the stark room she had been thrown into after her attack on Bel. There was only one door that was sealed shut. No windows...and other than her war fan, nothing to be used as a weapon. Listar's slaves had brought her clothes to change into but had taken away the yardage of her kimono and obi. They would have made a good noose.

She had briefly thought about ending her life in an honorable fashion so Listar couldn't use her against her loved ones. But then images of Daray flashed through her mind. For quite a while now her heart had fluttered every time the Nardo clan leader came near her. She had watched him since they had met. First, he was her captor. Later he became her friend. Over time she learned the character of the man, and somewhere along the way, she had fallen in love.

It was that love that stayed her hand. She had never told him what was in her heart. She didn't want to pass from this world with regrets, and not telling him how she felt would be the greatest regret of her life.

Suddenly a great noise startled Himeko out of her musings. A grinding noise was heard all around her. Himeko shifted to a stance that would better allow her to defend herself. Dust rained down from above, and Himeko looked up to see the ceiling sliding away.

"What in the five hells?" Staring down from a raised platform was Listar with a bloodthirsty grin on his face.

"Behold, gentlemen, the tiny princess with a warrior's soul," Listar called out like an event announcer.

Himeko scanned the darkened area above her. She was just able to make out several other shapes in the shadows.

"You invited us to watch the slaughter of

some insignificant female?" a voice in the darkness growled.

Listar's grin grew even bigger, "Just watch, my brother." He pulled a lever and the walls of Himeko's prison started to fall away. This part of Listar's palace could evidently do double duty changing between cells and a small arena. It didn't take long for Himeko to be standing alone in an open area with the spectators looking down on her.

Himeko heaved a sigh. It was so cliché that the entertainment was going to be violence in an arena. It seemed like every culture ran by the male of the species took enjoyment in the pain of others. If she survived this, she was going to take a vacation to Ludus Prime and get away from all of the testosterone for a while.

"You will be pitted against another slave this evening," Listar called down to Himeko. "You will be fighting for your life. They will be fighting for their freedom. If they manage to kill you, they are released from their bonds. If you kill them, you live to fight another day." Listar leaned over the platform wall to stare at Himeko intently. "Come on. Let me see more of your fire."

Himeko ignored him and tested the weight

and balance of the *tessen* in her hand. She moved through the familiar *kata* until her muscles remembered the movements ingrained in her since she was a child.

A door on the far side of the arena open and a man stepped through. He appeared to be a Kassian, his reptilian appearance giving away his species. It was just more proof that the Polaxians participated in the illegal slave trade. Kassis was one of the planets that outlawed slavery. According the galactic accords, enslaving people from species who banned slavery was illegal. Slaves were only to be bought and sold between the cultures who still allowed slavery on their planet.

Kassians were smaller than Polaxians or Vukasins, but their males still had the capacity to be heavily muscled and incredibly strong. This one appeared to be both. Most likely he had been serving his enslavement doing hard labor.

The Kassian took her measure while she looked him over. Himeko thought she saw a brief look of regret cross his scaled face before it settled into an unreadable mask. Her opponent raised his fists; each held a dagger-sized blade. Listar had ensured that this would be a battle of close contact with his choice of weapons.

Himeko had to decide to live or die in that moment. If she decided to live, then by default she also would decide to kill. He father's voice burst into her memory: "Only the strong survive. Are you strong or are you weak?"

Himeko straightened her spine and flicked the fan open to cover her face demurely. She inclined a bow of respect to the Kassian in front of her and then closed her *tessen* while she slid into a battle stance.

"I am strong," Himeko declared.

The two people in the arena stood frozen. Neither truly wanted to kill the other, but both knew that one of them wouldn't be leaving the arena alive. They stood like statues, their muscles bunched and ready to spring into action.

"Begin!" Listar shouted.

Himeko didn't move. After a brief pause, the Kassian launched himself at her with a roar. Himeko shifted to the side while deflecting his blade with her closed fan. The Kassian was aggressive in his attacks. Himeko remained on the defensive.

She could hear the jeers from the men in that audience, but she ignored them. They didn't matter;

only the battle in front of her mattered. Himeko narrowed her world to just the arena. To everyone else it appeared that the Kassian had the advantage, causing her to steadily retreat.

What they couldn't see was Himeko's mind analyzing the situation. She watched and learned. Every person favored certain attacks, and only the greatest masters were able to mask the little tells that would telegraph their next move. Himeko's father had been a strict task master. He taught her to use her mind instead of brute strength in battle.

Despite being on the defensive, Himeko's movements were graceful–almost like a dance. In comparison, the Kassian seemed hulking and slow. As the dance progressed, Himeko's movements slowly changed from strictly defense to a subtle offense. She tested her observations of the Kassians patterns, not enough to kill him, but enough to find out if he was willing to change his form when faced with a skilled fighter.

It turned out that the Kassian was brute strength, not a trained fighter. Even after several hits he continued to use the same patterns. All Himeko had to do was watch his footwork and his eyes and she could tell where he planned to land his next blow.

Himeko knew that to continue at this point would be folly. Even untrained fighters got lucky once in a while. The logical thing was to end it as soon as possible.

Himeko started landing hits meant to wear down her opponent. She saw the realization dawn in the Kassian's eyes. He was beginning to understand that he was not going to be the one who left the arena alive. As that fact sank in, his movements became more frantic and aggressive while Himeko remained calm and collected.

All this time, Himeko had been battling with a closed fan. She had used it like a blade to parry and thrust, the sharpened tines stabbing and cutting the Kassian until his body was covered in blood. The only blood covering Himeko was not her own.

The weakened Kassian stumbled and Himeko knew that was the point to end it swiftly. When the Kassian thrust the point of his blade towards her, she snapped open her *tessen* and tangled the blade in the spines. She twisted the fan, disarming that hand. The move brought the pair in close contact. The Kassian tried to recover by bringing his second blade to bear down on Himeko. She grabbed his wrist and used his own momentum to flip him onto the ground.

The disarmed Kassian lay at her feet, stunned.

"Finish it," he growled.

"I'm sorry," Himeko said.

The Kassian just closed his eyes as Himeko closed her fan and thrust it into the neck of the prone Kassian. He jerked in surprise and instinctively reached for his throat. Himeko used all of her strength to drag the fan through his flesh to sever the large artery most species seemed to have in their neck to carry oxygen to the brain.

The Kassian clutched Himeko's arm with wide eyes as his life's blood poured from his body. Himeko didn't look away as the life faded from the man's eyes. He deserved at least that respect. When his hand fell away and he drew his last breath, Himeko gently closed his eyes and stood.

She raised her chin as she flicked the blood from her battle fan.

"I am Himeko, daughter of the *kumicho* of the *Tsubaki-kai* and princess of the Nardo clan. Remember my name, for it will haunt you until the end of your days."

Listar stood clapping. "What a beautiful performance, my dear." He propped his elbow on the wall and rested his head in his chin in a nonchalant pose. "I think next time we will up the ante and see how you do against a trained opponent." He smiled. "I was worried that perhaps you had just landed a lucky blow against Bel. But here you stand without a single scratch and your adversary dead at your feet." Listar stood and laughed, "You should prove entertaining for a while."

The door at the end of the arena opened and several guards entered. Himeko tightened her grip on her war fan. It was times like this she wished she had a firearm. She was outnumbered, but she would take as many of the bastards with her as she could.

Listar had other ideas though. This was not meant to be another battle. He was simply reacquiring his possession. The guards advanced on her with raised shields. They boxed her in and limited her movement. She was able to land a few bruising blows, but she just didn't have the bulk to do much damage behind the shield.

When they had her immobilized, someone behind her hit her with an injection. She felt the sting of it and her vision started to blur. Her muscles didn't want to respond properly. Soon she was stumbling like a zoo animal hit with a tranquilizer. Of course that analogy wasn't far from the truth. She was a curiosity as far as the Polaxians were concerned. A delicate creature capable of defeating much strong opponents. She wouldn't be surprised if this whole farce was meant to study her and not just entertainment.

Himeko fell to the floor and struggled to move. She continued to claw her way across the floor even as her vision faded to black. The last thing she remembered was rough hands lifting her into the air as she lost all consciousness.

CHAPTER SIX

"Even dressed as a mercenary, your posture still screams Vukasin noble," Se'lak, the Kassian assisting them, said.

Daray shook his shoulders and tried to slump a little. It felt unnatural because rigid posture had been drilled into him at the imperial warrior's den. The Kassian slapped Daray's back and gave what passed for a grin on his reptilian face.

In the time it had taken the two ships to near the auction site, Daray had learned quite a bit about his new companion. Kavi had worked his contacts, but ultimately it was Zamira and Akia that had secured the help they needed. The ship that hailed them had been Kassian in design, and Se'lak was the captain, but it was manned by several different species, including Vukasin. The whole crew had one thing in common though, they had all been created in the lab that was discovered on Ludus Prime. They appeared to be a rag-tag group of outcasts that banded together as muscle for hire. The reality was far different.

Se'lak and his crew were fiercely loyal to the royal family of Ludus Prime. Zamira had made securing their freedom of choice, even from their genetic planets of origin, one of her primary objectives. She fought for them just as zealously as she did any other citizen of the planet. She had stood up against governments more powerful than her own, though Akia's fierce defense as well as his connections to Vukas had proved valuable. But Zamira was still able to earn the respect of many for her fairness and convictions. The fact that she fought for the rights of those that weren't even her species earned her admiration in many circles. It also earned the love and respect of those she defended. For that reason, many of those created by experiment had chosen to stay on Ludus Prime and make that planet their permeant home.

Se'lak and his crew delved into the darker side of interplanetary commerce. It was a role that allowed them to create an information network to rival the best spymasters. Even Kavi had said as much when he vouched for them.

"Come on," Se'lak urged. "We have to register for the auction before midday."

Daray picked up his pace. "Aren't they going to wonder how a poor group of mercenaries acquired enough wealth to buy so many slaves?"

Se'lak laughed, "Oh ye of little faith. I'm registering as proxy for a much wealthier individual. I saved his life once and he owed me. So should anyone check, my proxy is legit." He drew a phase gun at a nearby noise, startling Daray. It was just another shuttle being unloaded. "Just so you know, I will have to buy a few non-Vukasins to not raise questions," Se'lak continued as he holstered his gun.

Daray nodded thoughtfully. "I understand. Can you make most of those female?"

Se'lak narrowed his eyes at Daray. Daray realized how what he just said sounded and stuttered, "I just don't like the idea of a female being abused in slavery."

Se'lak stared at Daray for a moment longer. "I heard that you are on this mission to find your woman."

Daray sighed. "She is not my woman, though I do love her. If the twin moons bless me then one day she will choose to be mine."

Se'lak smiled, showing sharp pointed teeth. "Good answer. Come, let's go."

Daray wasn't used to being ordered around and had to remind himself that in this situation he was the subordinate. He dutifully followed a few paces behind the Kassian. It amazed Daray that the normally jovial male turned hard and menacing as they made their way through the crowd. Daray tried to copy his behavior, shoving people out of his way and growling down at those who got too close.

They were only a few yards away from the building where the auction was supposed to be held when a child attempted to pickpocket from Se'lak. The Kassian gave a roaring hiss and grabbed the youth, who appeared to be a Polaxian hybrid, probably a child the resulted from a master's abuse of a female slave. Because part of his bloodline was Polaxian, the child wasn't enslaved, but because he wasn't a pure blood he was considered a second-class citizen within the Polaxian empire. Such children were often thrown to the streets where only the strong survived.

Se'lak grabbed the struggling youth, who Daray estimated couldn't be more than ten cycles old. He tucked the child under his arm with an iron grip, ignoring the kicking and biting. They approached the doors of the auction house. The doors wouldn't be open for a few more hours, but their destination was the window off to one side.

A rheumy looking old man manned the window and barely glanced up as Se'lak and Daray's shadows crossed his window.

"The kid is part Polaxian. He can't be sold here. Your best bet would be just to kill him off and be done with it."

The child stilled and his skin paled beneath the dusting of fur covering his young face.

Se'lak leaned against the window and fished his proxy papers out with his free hand and plopped them in front of the old man. "If it comes to that I will, but I just happen to have need of a child to work in the engine ducts of my ship. Grown men are just too big."

The old man shrugged like it didn't matter to him one way or another. He picked up the papers and examined them. He used a crystal scanner to reveal the hidden seal that would prove this wasn't a forgery. He grunted which Daray took as a sign that the papers had passed inspection. The old man slapped a bidding bracelet onto Se'lak's wrist.

"You are allowed only one bodyguard on the floor." He looked Daray over before turning back to Se'lak. "At the end of the auction you will be given a time to retrieve your purchase. At that time you may bring the necessary manpower to control your merchandise. I suggest you bring your own control collars, or you can pay extra, they will be provided for you."

"Mark that we will pay the fee for the collars as my patron didn't have the foresight to provide them." Daray fought to keep his face impassive as Se'lak gave the order to the old man.

The man at the window nodded and made a notation on Se'lak's account.

"Next!" the old man bellowed, dismissing Se'lak and Daray.

Se'lak quickly made his way back towards their shuttle, still carrying a much more subdued youth. Daray may not be familiar with the shadowy world of spycraft, but he was intelligent enough not to demand answers until they were safely in their own shuttle.

As Se'lak shut and locked the shuttle doors, he set the child down.

"Please, my lord…let me go."

Se'lak scowled down at the child, making the boy visibly shake. "You tried to steal from me. You should consider yourself fortunate that I haven't killed you."

The young boy fidgeted, "I know, my lord, but…." His voice trailed off as tears collected in his eyes.

"Speak up boy!" Se'lak snapped. Even Daray cringed at the harshness in his voice.

"There's no one to protect her if I'm gone, sir."

"Protect who?" Daray asked.

The boy flicked his eyes between the two men towering over him. "M…m…my sister," he stuttered.

"Bring her here. I will have honest work for

both of you," Se'lak growled. "If you do not return I will hunt you down and punish you for your attempted theft."

The boy's tears cleared as he clenched his fists and glared at Se'lak. "I will not let you use my sister."

"Calm, boy," Daray said. "Your sister will be safer with us than she would be on the streets here."

The boy stared down Daray. "Promise?"

Daray kneeled down to the boy's level and extended his hand, "A promise between men. I'm Daray. What is your name, boy?"

The boy took Daray's hand and flushed. "I am just called boy."

Daray's heart ached at the thought of a child thrown away without even a name.

"A man should have a name," Se'lak declared. "Names have power. We shall call you Barin. It means 'noble warrior.' Do you think you can live up to such a name?"

The newly dubbed Barin thought before

nodding.

Se'lak opened the shuttle door.
"Go…retrieve your sister. Be back within the hour."

Barin scurried off and disappeared among the numerous shuttles docked for the auction.

"Do you think he will return?" Daray asked.

Se'lak closed the shuttle door looking thoughtful. "I hope so."

Daray sat in one of the chairs in the shuttle's common area. "You are a man of contradictions, Se'lak. One minute you pay to casually inflict pain on people and the next you are trying to rescue street urchins."

Se'lak order the ship to dispense a couple of rajia teas. He handed one steaming mug to Daray and sipped from the other. He sat down across from Daray and regarded the rather sheltered man.

"This is your first mission off of Vukas isn't it?"

"And so what if it is?" Daray demanded.

"Were you trained for covert work at all?"

Se'lak ignored Daray's statement about the slave collars, much to his chagrin.

"No. I am the clan leader for the Nardo."

Se'lak gave a soft whistle. "I was fairly certain you weren't trained for this, but I'm surprised they let such a high political official risk his neck in such a venture."

Daray flushed but didn't say anything. Se'lak studied him and then started to laugh.

"They didn't allow you to take on this mission did they?"

"Officially I stole a war ship and went rogue," Daray finally confessed.

Se'lak nodded and set his tea aside. "So you know that to accomplish what needs to be done you can't always do what is right?" Daray looked up at Se'lak and narrowed his eyes. "I know that those collars will inflict pain, and honestly I will activate at least one as we load the Vukasins onto our ship. It is what is expected from those who are controlling a multitude of slaves. Until we leave this obit, those people are to be treated as merchandise, not people. Which is worse? Temporary pain or a lifetime of slavery? Because if our ruse is discovered, those people will be sold to someone else."

Daray sighed. "You've made your point, and I understand why you did what you did."

"I'm glad you have more intelligence than most politicians." Se'lak smiled and picked his tea back up. He leaned back in his seat and regarded Daray. "You are a pretty well-known figure on Vukas, aren't you?"

"All clan leaders are."

"I thought so." Se'lak sighed, "We are going to have to do something about your appearance. Otherwise the captives might accidently betray us. How good are you with using double energy swords?"

"The *kijani-a* of the Vukasin Empire has been the only one to defeat me when sparring."

"Could you kill if you had to?"

Daray nodded.

"Good. I think I have an excellent disguise for you." They were interrupted as a knock sounded at the shuttle door.

Se'lak drew his weapon and stood to the side as Daray checked the monitor. Barin appeared in the visual as well as a small cloaked bundle next to him that Daray assumed was his sister. Se'lak motioned for Daray to open the shuttle door but didn't relinquish his weapon.

When the door opened, a youth, much older but still maybe only a teenager, rushed into the shuttle, only to be confronted with Se'lak's pulse gun.

The youth held up his hands and stood still. Daray noticed that behind him, in addition to Barin and his sister, were probably a half dozen youths of varying age, all male save for the cloaked bundle that they had in their center standing next to Barin.

The oldest was the one who had entered first and was now staring down Se'lak's gun.

"Boy...I mean Barin, said you had work for him and the girl." The youth looked Se'lak in the eyes even as he tried to hide the tremble of his legs.

"That's right. I have offered them positions as part of my crew."

The youth sneered. "Many others have offered to take our sister. What makes you any different?"

Se'lak holstered his gun, "Because me and mine believe that young ones, especially females, should be protected. What I offer is honest work. It won't always be easy, and the days will be long, but no one will abuse them, not while any of us draw breath."

For the first time since Daray opened the shuttle door, the dull eyes of the gathered children shined with a bit of hope.

A boy in the back of the protective circle took off his hat and called out, "You wouldn't happen to have need of a few more of us, my lord?"

Se'lak turned to Daray in silent question because they both knew that the dangerous nature of Se'lak's work meant that Daray would have to take charge of the children. All of them were hybrids of Polaxian and various other species, though most seemed to be a mix of Vukasin, Ludian and possibly even human. Daray gave a small nod. He couldn't let the children suffer if he might have a chance to help them.

"Come in." Se'lak turned back into the shuttle. "We will eat and discuss terms."

At the mention of food, the children rushed into the shuttle.

CHAPTER SEVEN

"Stop fidgeting with that damn mask," Se'lak growled under his breath at Daray.

"How do the Touling assassins breathe through this thing?" Daray replied.

"It is meant for intimidation, not comfort. They are known for their stoicism." Se'lak slapped his hand away from his face. "You are going to give the ruse away if you can't play the part."

Daray sobered immediately. He would not be the reason that they were unable to save his kinsmen. His hands went to his sides, hidden beneath the dark cloak that covered his armor and double swords. The hood left his eyes shrouded in darkness while the lower half of his face was covered with a leather mask fashioned to look like some fierce monster. Daray had to admit that the whole look was intimidating.

Se'lak played the part of hired proxy for the auction. Daray was to play the part of bodyguard. Se'lak assured him that the Touling disguise wouldn't be out of place, as the organization was made up of several species and were known to take whatever job paid. Their honor fell more in their reputation of completing every job or dying in the attempt. Even if you offered to pay a Touling more to leave a job they never would. However, once the job was completed they had no qualms in returning and killing a former master if someone paid them for it.

As Se'lak and Daray approached the auction house, the entire atmosphere of the outpost changed. Evidently auction nights were almost like carnivals to the residents of the outpost. Several vendors lined the road leading to the auction house. Brightly colored banners flew while music played on the wind.

Even children weaved through the massive crowds. Daray still wasn't sure about Se'lak's decision to give each of the children a little bit of money to partake in the night's festivities while gathering information, but he had to concede that the children wouldn't seem out of place in the crowd.

Two burly Polaxians stopped Se'lak at the door of the auction house. He raised his arm to show the bidding bracelet attached to his wrist.

The Polaxian guard on the left grunted but growled, "Blasters, pulse weapons, projectile weapons are forbidden beyond this point. We will have to search you before entering."

Se'lak gave a reptilian grin, "I have no problems being searched, but," he thumbed over to Daray, "he might have a problem with it."

Daray rolled the cloak back from his shoulders, revealing the intricate pair of swords strapped to either hip that denoted the Touling organization. He placed his hands lightly on the hilt of each and shifted his weight into a battle stance. The movement was subtle, but it changed the atmosphere of the interaction completely. Those waiting in line to enter the auction house behind Se'lak took a step back. A circle of quiet enveloped Daray and the guards. Daray's lips quirked behind his mask as he saw the Polaxian guard that challenged them take an involuntary step back.

Daray was almost disappointed when the guards waved them through without any more confrontation. Se'lak explained as they found their assigned table that Polaxians never went anywhere without a bladed weapon of some sort, so they never forbid the old fashioned weapons.

Soon the doors to the auction house closed and the lights dimmed. Daray noticed that every server delivering food and drinks to the tables wore the shock collar so many slave owners preferred. It allowed the masters to dole out punishment even from a distance. If the individual with the control chose, he could also kill at a distance.

Daray grabbed the hand of a pretty young woman who placed the glass of water he had requested in front of him. She turned dull and dead eyes on him. Daray released her hand without a word. He knew that even if he was miraculously able to rescue her from this place that she had already been broken beyond repair.

Daray had stayed out of intergalactic politics for the most part. If it hadn't affected the Nardo, he had been content to let Ghaleb and the others make those decisions. But the more he saw of the slave trade firsthand, the more it made his blood boil. If Ghaleb didn't imprison him for treason when he returned, Daray was going to make sure that the Nardo no longer stood by the wayside when it came to the rest of the galaxy.

Another slave entered the stage. He appeared to be a male from Ludus Prime. In a monotone voice, he acted as the announcer for the proceedings. Daray was surprised to see several humans on the auction block, both male and female. Evidently the Tanis continued to pillage that distant planet to fill their coffers.

Se'lak bid on several of the human females, even winning a few. Daray wanted to demand that he keep pushing the bids up higher until all of the women were safe, but he knew that would draw undue attention to him. He did take note of who won each human. He would pass that information on to Megan and Reijo later. Hopefully they might be able to recover them.

The format of the auction seemed to be physically weaker species first. These were meant to be household servants and menial labor. The humans and Ludians mostly fell into this category with a few other species. Next came the strong but easily controlled slaves. Many of these were from worlds much lower on the evolutionary scale, where they would react mostly like trained beasts. A few of the Tanis deformed experiments found themselves on the auction block, forever frozen in their warped bestial state. Last came the strong and cunning. These were to be handled with care. Most were destined for the gladiatorial arenas or the front lines of a war not of their making.

Soon the missing Vukasins came to the block. Se'lak had to lay a restraining hand on Daray's shoulder as the auctioneer demonstrated how the elite Vukasin warriors would make superior gladiators by using the slave collars to inflict so much pain on them that they transformed into their battle beasts.

Daray had to watch in silent horror as one of the youngest members of that ship's crew was forced to transform. The young man evidently felt that an almost certain death was preferable to a life as a slave because he used tooth and claw to eviscerate the announcer, which demonstrated why they used a slave for such a function. He charged towards the audience before his handler activated the slave collar at an even higher setting. The shock knocked the young Vukasin to his knees, but he got back up and continued to fight. Three more times he was knocked to the ground. Each time he seemed to become more rabid, the pain and loss of freedom driving him mad. In the end, the handler decided to cut his losses and used a lethal dose of energy the final time.

Daray watched the life go out of the eyes of a young man that he recognized as a Nardo youth. Dara had pinned the young man's commission insignia on his uniform right before his assignment to Himeko's diplomatic mission. Now that youth lay dead just a few yards away because he wouldn't submit to a life of slavery. It was such a waste of a strong passionate life.

Daray's hands clenched against the hilts of the swords at his side. It took every ounce of willpower not to blow their cover by charging the stage and killing off as many of the slavers as he could before they took him out. The only thing that stayed his hand was the knowledge that if he gave in to the bloodlust it would doom the rest of the people they were trying to rescue.

In the end, they had purchased all but three of the missing Vukasin crew members. Se'lak joked with the other buyers. He had them convinced that his employer was looking to create a new stable of gladiators and a breeding program after seeing the Vukasin Beast before the resort on Ludus Prime had ceased its operations. The Vukasins, along with the human females, were going to be the basis of his breeding program. It disgusted Daray to listen to those people casually debate the cost effectiveness of such a venture.

Of the three missing crew members, one was the youth that died before their eyes, the other two were Himeko and an engineer. The auction ended without a sign of Himeko. Daray's heart dropped. She wasn't with the rest of the missing crew. He refused to accept the possibility that she might be dead. He just knew that if she no longer lived he would have felt that loss in his soul.

Daray silently stood with Se'lak as the lights raised. He could puzzle out where Himeko was after they got the rest of their people safely aboard the Kassian vessel. Se'lak played the dutiful proxy for a wealthy buyer. He inspected their purchases close up to insure health. The poor human women nearly fainted at the sight of the reptilian alien. It was difficult for Daray to remain silent as the farce continued, but he pulled on his willpower to finish playing his part. Se'lak declared himself satisfied with the merchandise and transferred the exorbitant amount of credits to the auction house owners, who would distribute the price of the slaves to the various slavers after taking their percentage.

Se'lak and Daray left to hurry back to their

shuttle, where the street children waited for them. The auction house would use the ship coordinates that Se'lak gave to slipstream the slaves directly into the ship's cargo hold. Se'lak wanted the shuttle back aboard the ship so they could leave orbit as soon as the transfer was complete.

Daray wanted to be there to see if he could find out any information regarding Himeko. After seeing with his own eyes the lot of slaves, Daray was determined to find Himeko as soon as possible. He only prayed he wasn't too late. He told himself that Himeko may appear delicate but she had a core of strength inside of her.

CHAPTER EIGHT

Himeko cracked open an eye to confirm that she was once again awoken because Listar came into her holding cell. Himeko feigned sleep. Each night the hungry look on Listar's face seemed to get more intense. She knew that one night her captor wasn't going to leave and one of them would end up not leaving the cell alive because she refused to submit to rape.

Thankfully Listar left her cell, locking the door behind him. Himeko rolled over and stared at the bare ceiling. Her days were beginning to run together in her windowless cell. She was only able to mark time by the food they served her and the times she was pulled to fight for Listar's entertainment.

A tear escaped Himeko's eye as she blinked away the weakness. Such senseless deaths. Maybe her father had been right. He always said that as a woman she would be too soft for the brutality of running the *Tsubaki-kai*. The faces of the slaves she had been forced to fight and kill haunted her dreams. She was discovering that she wasn't capable of being a cold-blooded killer.

That knowledge made her reexamine her past decisions. She had fled her father's home in anger because he was arranging a marriage with the son of another organization's leader. Their union was supposed to cement an alliance which would have given control of all of Tokyo's underworld to one unified organization. She had been angry that her father hadn't even consulted her about the proposal. But it was his declaration that she would never take over and that he had to find a man to run the family business that had caused her to drive away in a huff. Ultimately, she would have submitted to her father's will; she was after all a properly raised Japanese daughter, but she needed to release her anger and frustration.

That was how she found herself at the desolate shrine just outside of the city. Before her mother had passed away, she had regularly taken Himeko there just to get away from the bustle of the city. Himeko often went there to think, and that night was no different in the beginning.

She had given her offering and rung the bell to wake the resident gods. While her head was bowed in prayer, she had felt large strong hands grab her. As the darkness descended, she had thought her father's enemies had found her and kicked herself for ditching her bodyguards. It wasn't until she woke up on Vukas that she had discovered that it wasn't her father's enemies that grabbed her.

For a while there, Himeko had prepared herself for an honorable suicide because she would never allow a man to violate her. She wasn't a prude, but she strongly believed in choice. It was one of the reasons she was so angry with her father the day she was kidnapped, because she felt that he had taken away her choices.

It had been a couple of years since she had been taken from Earth. Vukas now felt like home. The people of the Nardo clan treated her with respect that bordered on reverence. Her thoughts and opinions were respected and her voice was heard. She was helping to create the world instead of just passing through it. Honestly, she hardly thought of her former life on Earth. She had found a purpose besides being a pretty accessory.

Himeko sighed. It sounded like she hadn't loved her family, but that wasn't true. In fact she deeply cared for her family. She also knew that if she just reappeared after years that it would dishonor her family name. It was better if she remained dead to them.

Was that the only reason she wanted to stay on Vukas? No. A certain clan chieftain with dark brooding eyes and a quiet strength popped into her memory. Daray of the Nardo. She wasn't sure when she fell in love with him. It wasn't the sudden attraction that her friend Megan had experienced with Reijo. It had built slowly over time. It started as grudging respect that turned into a solid friendship. Soon she found herself looking forward to the time she spent with Daray.

She had always hoped that he would declare his love to her one day, but he never did. It took the Polaxian attack to force Himeko to examine her own feelings. Even if Daray never fell in love with her, Himeko realized that she would regret never telling him how she felt. It was why she fought so desperately to stay alive now. She didn't want to leave this life with regrets.

Himeko tried to get comfortable on the thin cot mattress. She needed to rest or her reflexes would suffer and that could end her life if Listar put her in another fight. So she closed her eyes and used an old trick from her childhood. She created a story in her mind and made herself the main character. It was a way to get her mind to quit worrying long enough to fall asleep. It also had the added benefit of the story often carrying over into her dreams.

Tonight she placed herself at the beautiful little cove on the Vukasin sea shore. It was a secluded area that one wouldn't find unless you knew it was there. Daray had taken her there once and she had been enchanted with the beauty of the place. So in her imagination tonight she was lying on the beach as the sun set. The clear night bloomed and the twin moons of Vukas shone so brightly that she needed no light to see the details of the cove.

Himeko was tired of being alone, so she created a figure to join her there in the imaginary cove. As the figure neared her, the features of Daray came into focus. In her mind, Himeko was able to be bold instead of proper. She reached for Daray and pulled him down into the sand next to her. She stared at his dark fathomless eyes before leaning over to kiss him.

Himeko drifted off into sleep with a smile on her face as she imagined the loving scene between her and Daray.

CHAPTER NINE

Daray paced back and forth across the cargo hold of *The Revenge*. Se'lak had agreed to take the human women and street children back to Ludus Prime. They had offered to take the Vukasin crew that they had rescued back as well. A few chose to go, but many of the crew of the diplomatic mission were of the Nardo clan. The clan after all had a close relationship with Vukasin ships—first the seafaring vessels and now those that navigated the stars.

Just as the crew that volunteered to steal the warship to save the woman they consider the clan princess, those rescued Nardo wanted to be a part of the search for Himeko as well. They didn't care that they may be labeled traitors upon return to Vukas;

Himeko was that important to them. Her grace and beauty gave them hope. Her natural consideration and compassion made everyone love her. But they admired her strength the most. Nearly everyone in the Nardo clan considered her the perfect female representation of the clan. It was one of the reasons that when the people of the stronghold learned that her name held the meaning of 'princess' on her home planet that they started referring to her as the Nardo Princess. The name stuck until she became a symbol for the entire clan.

"Are you sure?" Daray demanded.

The navigational officer of the diplomatic mission, called Anjum, answered, "As sure as I could be without navigational charts to double check. The star configuration when they first unloaded us from the Polaxian ship led me to believe that we were on the Polaxian main home world."

"Damn. Flying a warship into that orbit would be a declaration of war. If she had been offloaded on one of the outer planets it could have been brushed off as a rogue raid." Daray continued his pacing. His only clue to Himeko's whereabouts was the last place the rest of the crew had seen her. "And that was where Raylan disappeared?"

Raylan was the missing crew member. He had been Daray's childhood friend.

"We were unloaded near the sea shore. They had us lined up on the beach with captives from other species. The Polaxians were dividing us into various ships for transport to different sites. Some captives had already been sold and were being transported to their new owners while many of the others were headed to different auction sites based on buyer preferences." Anjum was proving to be a very observant officer with a cool head despite his young years. Daray made note to keep an eye on the man.

Anjum continued, "Our auction seemed to be slated for pleasure entertainment: Gladiators, beautiful women and effeminate men for the brothels. Vukasins are very popular for the arenas since they appear so rarely."

"Then why wasn't Himeko with you? You can't deny she is an exotically beautiful woman."

Anjum sighed, "She was never slated for sale. The leader of the raid was a man by the name of Listar. He claimed her before the ship even landed."

Things just kept getting worse and worse. Megan had given Daray information on the Polaxian royal family with the thought that he might be able to appeal to them to help locate Himeko. They knew that the Polaxians had allied themselves with the Tanis, but Vukas was still considered a powerful enemy. They had hoped that they would consider it more prudent to help the Vukasins rather than give them cause to start a war. Unfortunately, Daray recognized the name Listar from the records of the royal family, and since in Polaxian culture certain names were reserved strictly for the royal family it wouldn't be the case that this Listar was someone different.

If the royal family enslaved the diplomat of Vukas, then Daray could assume that they would be no help in her retrieval. *Frex.* What were they going to do now?

"Tell me what happened to Raylan." Daray changed the subject. He would have to carefully consider his next move.

"I honestly don't know what happened. We were lined up on the beach, shackled together waiting for whatever came next. One minute we were all there…the next we heard Raylan scream, but when we looked he wasn't there."

"A shackled man doesn't just disappear.'

"His shackles had been broken clean through and the only sign was drag marks leading to the sea. Whatever got him had to be impossibly quick otherwise we would have seen it."

"How did your Polaxian captors react?"

Anjum thought about it. "Surprisingly calm, if somewhat put out. I heard them complaining that Raylan was the third slave lost in the last two weeks. Some of the lower-caste Polaxians even complained that the royals should do something about the creature devouring their stock."

"Creature? So Raylan is dead?" Daray's voice cracked slightly with the question.

Anjum sighed. "That seemed to be the consensus from the Polaxians. I am not familiar with their native flora and fauna so I couldn't say for certain."

Daray turned to the computer console in the cargo bay. He directed it to pull up any records of biological life on Polax. He started narrowing the search parameters to predators, then sea dwelling, etc. While he found several large sea-based predators they tended to stay in deep open water. He could find no documentation for a creature that snatched its prey from land. It didn't mean that one didn't exist, but it was a good indication that the Polaxians didn't know what they were dealing with either.

Daray punched the bulkhead. It didn't really matter at this point. His friend was gone. What he needed to do was devise a strategy that would allow him to rescue Himeko. He was out of his realm of experience. He needed to consult with someone who knew how to navigate covert operations. His first choice would have been Kavi but the old buzzard-raptor had already sent word through Se'lak that because of the tenuous nature of diplomatic relations with the Polaxian government he could do nothing for Daray. But Se'lak might be able to help. The Kassian of Ludus Prime had spent much more time navigating the shadows than he had.

He waved good bye to Anjum. His crew could get the new members settled. He needed to get to a secure line to see if Se'lak would even listen to him. Daray may be a proud man, but he was intelligent enough to ask for help when he was out of his depth.

CHAPTER TEN

"I don't like this," Daray growled at Baldar, his new companion. He tugged at the stolen uniform he was wearing. "I feel like a traitor in this thing."

Baldar chuckled. He was one of the Vukasin experiments on Ludus Prime and was now a part of Se'lak's crew. Daray observed that he seemed perfectly comfortable in the Tanis uniform. It might have something to do with the fact that the Vukasins born of the experiment didn't have specific clan ties. In fact, there was talk of allowing them to form their own clan, though no one was sure how that would be accomplished since it came to light that Megan deactivated the temple complex in the carnivorous jungle on Vukas. So the debate raged instead of moving forward.

"Se'lak was able to tap into communications between Bel and various royal Polaxian entities. Listar, as the youngest son, is hosting the Tanis contingency." Baldar turned to Daray with a serious look on his face. "If you can't do this, I need to know now. I can call one of my brothers down to act as my backup."

"I can do what needs to be done," Daray sighed. "Though I am gaining a new respect for your crew's adaptability. You all seem to be able to change quicker than a specter-bug."

Baldar flashed a handsome grin, falling into the character they had settled on. Daray and Baldar were supposed to play the part of newly transferred soldiers. Baldar would be the playboy who liked to drink and party, while Daray was his sober and somewhat somber friend that kept him from going too far.

They were in the port town near the coast of Polax's southern continent. Listar's compound was just outside of the city. It was his duty as the local royal to make sure nothing disturbed the flow of trade. All slaves were brought here to be listed into inventory before heading to various buyers and auctions. The royal family took a percentage of every slave listed.

"Let's go there."

Baldar pointed to a rowdy tavern and Daray frowned. He wanted to get information about Himeko, not get drunk.

"There. That look right there is perfect, D." Baldar clapped Daray on the back and steered him towards the tavern.

Daray continued to frown as he leaned against the bar slowly sipping on his ale. He watched as Baldar worked the room. Daray had to admit the man was good. Baldar had gone from stranger to best buddies with the other Tanis soldiers in less than an hour. Soon, between drink and comradery, Baldar was gathering the information that the pair needed to locate Himeko.

"D! D! Get over here," a drunk-appearing Baldar called.

Daray slowly unfolded himself from his leaning position on the bar and walked over to the jovial Baldar. As he neared, Daray noticed that Baldar may be acting drunk but his eyes were clear of the typical glazed look that a man lost in his cups would have.

Baldar slapped Daray on the back, nearly

knocking him into the table filled with Tanis soldiers.

"Guys," Baldar slurred, "This dour fellow is my friend, D. He's a bit of a stick in the mud but…but…" Baldar threw his arms around Daray's neck, "I love you, man."

The table snickered as Daray extracted himself from Baldar's embrace. Playing the part of long-suffering friends, he said, "Someone has to make sure your drunk ass gets back to the barracks."

Baldar suddenly turned sloshing his drink everywhere. "Oh, tell D about that female you were talking about."

Daray sighed, "I am not dragging you out of a pleasure house again to make sure you report for duty on time."

A burly Tanis soldier laughed, "Not that kind of female, friend. This one would eviscerate you before ever giving your rod a ride."

Daray knew the sexism that the Tanis fostered among its males, so he snorted. "Are you saying you aren't man enough to handle a single female?"

The Tanis soldier's face flushed red. "Perhaps you should keep your opinions to yourself until you see her in action. Cold as ice, she is, and doesn't even flinch when she lands the killing blow."

Daray took a seat at the table, "She must be a decidedly unfeminine woman."

The Tanis soldier picked up his ale and threw back a drink. He said as he wiped his lips, "That is where you would be wrong, friend. She is a delicate little thing with long black hair that shines blue when the light hits it just right. Her skin is so pale that when the blood spatters on it the contrast feels obscene. She moves like she is dancing...." The man's voice trailed off as he remembered the deadly beauty.

Daray's heart stuttered. With the exception of the cold disregard for life, that description sounded a lot like Himeko.

"I don't believe you," sneered Daray.

"Then see her for yourself." The Tanis soldier slammed his ale on the table. "She is a slave to the Polaxian prince that oversees this area. He likes to put her on show in the arena from time to time."

"When is the next show?" Baldar asked.

"Tomorrow night."

*****

The arena was smaller than Daray would have thought. But then again, it was part of a private residence rather than a public stadium complex. Baldar and Daray stood in the shadows near the entrance. They had been informed by the Polaxian guards that they would only be allowed in if there was room. Elite citizens and guests of the royal family had preference, lowly foreign soldiers ranked barely above the peasantry.

Daray couldn't keep from fidgeting. Everything in him was itching to run through the building searching for Himeko. The only thing keeping him from blowing their cover was the infuriatingly calm presence of Baldar. He was evidently used to the hurry up and wait that occurred with so many missions.

Daray closed his eyes and concentrated on his breathing. It was a trick his old instructor taught his students. He counted his breaths in and out, lengthening them each time. His heart rate began to slow and his body relaxed. The nervous energy flowed out with each breath until he was once again the calm and collected Daray that he was known for.

When Daray opened his eyes once more, he saw the guards closing the doors without letting them in.

"Five hells!"

Daray marched towards the closing doors with the intent to demand entrance when Baldar grabbed his shoulder to stop him. Daray spun around with a growl. Baldar laid a finger to his lips, indicating silence. He pulled Daray further into the shadows as they rounded the building that housed the arena.

"Always have a contingency plan," Baldar whispered to Daray. He then guided them to a service door that had slaves carrying patters of food and drink from the main house to the guests at the arena. "Our drunk friend warned me after you left that we probably wouldn't get in because we were lowly soldiers. Social standing holds a lot of sway on this planet, it is practically a caste system. But he did say that the servant's entrance rarely had a guard posted so it was fairly easy to sneak in."

Daray and Baldar wove their way through the

bustling slaves, who basically ignored their presence. They followed the roar of the crowd to make their way towards the arena proper. Daray stood in a doorway. Every seat in the small arena was filled. This had evidently become a rather popular pastime. The lights dimmed around the audience as the arena floor was illuminated with a spotlight.

Out walked a mean-looking, muscular Kassian man with the telltale collar of a slave around his neck. He paced around the arena. The Kassian roared and hissed, working the crowd into a frenzy. The sound of stomping feet, cheers and jeers was deafening.

Into that din walked a stately delicate woman with long black hair and exotic slanted eyes. Daray would recognize the graceful sway of her delicate hips anywhere. It was Himeko. Her quiet presence was such a sharp contrast to the posturing of her opponent.

Daray took a moment to drink in the sight of her. Even in the utilitarian jumpsuit she seemed almost regal. In one hand she carried a fan. Daray's temper simmered at the thought that she was thrown out there to battle a man twice her size who had a sword, unarmed. Listar was obviously trying to kill her off. The emotionless mask that Himeko wore told Daray that she had accepted that fate.

A Polaxian stood on the far platform and was illuminated with a spotlight. Daray assumed that this must be the Prince Listar.

"Friends and honored guests," he quieted the crowd with his booming voice. "I Welcome you to this display of battle prowess."

A voice in the crowd called out with a guffaw, "More like livestock to slaughter!" The crowd around him laughed at the joke as Listar inclined a head towards the voice.

"Perhaps, but let us see which animal dies tonight." With that, Listar left the spotlight to return to his seat.

Daray turned his attention back to the arena floor. Himeko had always been a reserved person, but there was something downright glacial about her standing there. It was as if she had locked away all of her emotions and personality.

"Begin!"

The Kassian flew into a whirlwind of movement. Himeko shifted her stance slightly and opened her fan, placing it in front of her. She watched her opponent like he was a bug trapped in glass.

She waved her fan in an almost hypnotic movement and Daray recalled watching her practice a dance with a fan she called a *kata* back at the stronghold. At the time, he had simply thought it was an elegant dance from her home world. Now he was beginning to understand that it wasn't just a dance.

The Kassian charged Himeko and she used her fan to deflect the blade of her attacker. Her movements still reminded him of a dance, but he could now see that dance was training for muscle memory when it came to battle.

With every twist, turn and attack, Himeko's facial expression never changed. It was as if part of her was missing from the battle. Soon the overconfident Kassian was on the defensive and was making mistakes. Daray could see Himeko watching and waiting for just the right moment.

Finally the Kassian made a fatal mistake with an aggressive attack. Himeko ducked beneath his reach, unfurled her fan and sliced it across his neck just above the slave collar. The Kassian grabbed his neck in a futile effort to stem the flow of his life's blood spraying from the severed artery. Himeko just stood there with dispassionate eyes watching the life leave him. Even dripping from the blood of the life she just took, her expression never changed.

Daray feared that Listar had somehow taken away a vital part of the woman he loved.

"Himeko!" Daray had a death grip on the rail of the fence surrounding the seating of the arena. He only realized that he had shouted for her out loud when the rest of the arena fell silent and Himeko turned towards him.

"Vukas spy!" Listar bellowed, "Secure him!"

Polaxian guards started running towards them as Baldar hauled Daray away from the railing.

"Do you even know the meaning of covert work?" Baldar groused as they dodged various slaves.

Daray ignored him. "I have to get to Himeko."

Baldar just shook his head. "One track mind…come on. I got directions to the floor."

"What do we do when we get there?" Daray

asked as he punched out a man who tried to grab him with one had as he pulled his sword free with the other.

"I'm kind of making this up as we go," Baldar admitted while dispatching his own opponent. "But I sort of have an idea?"

"Sort of?" Daray and Balder burst through a door and found themselves on the arena floor.

CHAPTER ELEVEN

Himeko's emotionless mask slipped when she heard Daray call her name. For a moment she thought it was simply wishful thinking until the arena erupted into chaos. She tracked Daray as another Vukasin in a Tanis uniform pulled him out of her line of sight. She searched the crowd hoping to find them again.

Thankfully, Listar seemed so preoccupied with finding Daray that he forgot to have her returned to confinement. Himeko was stuck in the arena for the time being, but at least she had room to fight and weapons to fight with.

She kept her *tessen* in one hand while she picked up the sword of the fallen Kassian—another senseless death for the entertainment of despicable people. The sword was sturdy if somewhat poorly balanced, but it would do for now.

Himeko turned to defend herself when the arena doors flew open. Instead she rushed into the arms of Daray with tears streaming down her face. She kissed him soundly, which left his eyes wide with wonder.

"Hate to break up the love fest, but we have company," a man that Himeko did not know said.

Daray kept one arm around Himeko but turned to face the other man and the slaves and soldiers that were massing behind him.

"Baldar, now might be a good time to try out that plan of yours." Daray pushed Himeko behind his back and got into a battle stance.

Himeko didn't stay in his protection, however. She stepped out with her weapons drawn to stand as his equal beside him.

"What is this plan?" Himeko asked as she dispatched a soldier that got too close.

The man known as Baldar gave her a cheeky grin and pulled out a device.

"This is a little thing that my boss cooked up," Baldar said as he pushed a button.

Himeko felt the slave collar around her neck give a click as it unlocked and fell off her neck. She reached up to feel her newly bare neck when she realized that she heard several metallic clanks as other collars fell to the ground.

She looked all around to see a multitude of slaves standing in shock as their collars fell to the ground. Soon the slaves realized that they were no longer in danger of punishment or death from those damned collars and quickly turned on their masters. Many knew they would still die, but at least in that moment they would die free men.

The chaos that ensued gave the trio a chance to slip away from the battle. They wove themselves through the maze of corridors until they found themselves outside of the arena.

"We have to get back to the seashore. That is our extraction point," Baldar called on the run.

Himeko struggled to keep up with the long-legged Vukasins, but she refused to ask them to slow down. She wanted off this planet as much as they did.

They had just made it to the beach when a set of soldiers caught up with them. Unlike the men within the arena who had been relegated to ceremonial swords, these guys had phase guns and stunners. They evaded fire as best they could.

Baldar's body jerked as a phase blast hit him and his body fell to the ground. The fallen man groaned in pain as Daray and Himeko dragged him behind a rock outcrop. Himeko noticed Daray frantically searching Baldar's uniform.

"What are you looking for?"

"Kavi had our people reverse engineer the personal slipstream device that Banji brought back. All of his operatives now carry one in case of emergency. Baldar may be a Ludian operative, but I'm fairly certain...there it is!" Daray held up a small crystal device and slapped it on Baldar's chest. He hit the device and then shoved Himeko away and covered her with his body.

With a whoosh of displaced air and a pop like thunder, the injured Baldar disappeared.

"Why didn't we get into the stream?" Himeko asked.

"We were only able to engineer the device to

be able to carry enough latent energy to carry one person, one way, one time. It would have killed us all if we had tried to ride it out with him."

"So what do we do now?"

Daray shrugged and Himeko sighed. Well, even if they didn't escape, at least she could tell him how she felt so she could die without regret.

"Daray, I lo—"

"Do you know how much trouble you are causing me you old mangy rhino-bear?" a familiar voice interrupted them.

"Raylan?" Daray jumped up and embraced the stranger, only to duck behind the rocks once again when their enemy fired on them. "I thought you were dead?"

"You should know I am not that easy to kill." Raylan bowed to Himeko. "Princess, I was on my way to rescue you, but it seems my old friend beat me to the punch."

The rock protecting them splintered with another phase blast.

"Well, I'm not going to say no if you want to

lend a hand at the moment," Daray laughed.

CHAPTER TWELVE

Himeko followed behind the two men. Raylan was leading them out into the open towards the water. For a moment she wondered if he had betrayed them as the guards closed in on them.

"Cover your eyes!" Raylan cried as he turned to throw something.

Himeko almost didn't follow his directions, but when a light that rivaled the sun flashed behind her closed eyelids, she was glad that in the end she chose to trust her former crew member. He had lobbed some sort of flash grenade at the oncoming guards.

Himeko opened her eyes and looked behind

her to see the disoriented Polaxians running into each other or falling to the ground. Suddenly, her world was engulfed in darkness as a metallic container of some sort snapped closed around her. She screamed and beat at walls enclosing her. She had been so close to escape, but she hadn't counted on the Polaxians having traps around the area for escaped slaves.

She wouldn't go back. She refused to return to the life of a slave. She thought back on Daray. He had come for her; that must mean something. And she had kissed him. It wasn't exactly the declaration of love she wanted to give him, but even if she died, at least he would know that she felt more than just respect for him.

Himeko calmed her breathing and prepared herself to attack as soon as the pod she was in was opened. She could feel that they were on the move, as she had to concentrate to keep her balance. When her mind cleared of her initial panic, she could hear a soft whooshing noise outside of the pod. She had to pop her ears as the pressure changed. Where were they taking her?

Himeko used one hand to brace herself against the wall of the pod as something hit the outside of her small prison. She was shocked to have her hand come away wet with water. She looked around the pod and noticed that water was leaking all around the seam where the pod closed around her. Another hit to the pod had her stumbling.

Dear god, she was underwater…fairly deep considering the pressure change. Did the Polaxians dump her in the ocean to dispose of her? What happened to Daray and Raylan? Something struck the pod even harder this time. The water coming in went from a minor seepage to a steady flow. It was collecting in the bottom of the pod and already it was past her ankles. At this rate she would only have a few more minutes before the entire pod was full of water. Drowning was definitely not how she wanted to die.

She could feel the pod's movement increase in speed. If this was a death sentence it was an effectively torturous one. If the pod sank to the bottom of the sea intact, the prisoner was left to die lone from suffocation once the air was used up in the pod or dehydration, whichever came first. If the pod was damaged like hers, they died of drowning. Himeko would much prefer a quick death at the end of a blade given a choice.

The water was now up to her waist. It took

every ounce of self-discipline Himeko had to keep from panicking. Himeko found herself underwater when the stop of her descent knocked her off balance. She came up sputtering and was just righting herself when the water sloshed as the pod moved to the side with a metallic grinding.

Himeko pulled her *tessen* free. Her intuition told her that she wasn't going to die drowning in the pod after all.

The pod cracked open, spilling both the water and Himeko to the floor. Strange hands grabbed at her and she used her closed fan to crack across their wrist as she rolled away from them to land in a battle stance.

Her soaked clothes were uncomfortable, and the minerals from the sea left her skin itchy, but she refused to give in to her discomfort. Her eyes scanned the shocked crowd surrounding her. It was filled with unfamiliar Polaxian faces as well as a few other races. It appeared that Listar had captured her again.

Attack or defend? She would probably last longer on the defensive. But she didn't plan on surviving this altercation. She would never live as a slave again. She had no regrets anymore after kissing Daray.

Her eyes scanned the crowd and landed on a large, stately looking Polaxian that everyone seemed to defer to. She was fairly certain that he was one of the royal family, as they were the only Polaxians that she had ever seen with black tipping the mane of golden hair that surrounded their heads.

She shifted in preparation for the attack. The royal Polaxian noticed her movement and, instead of calling guards and slaves over to protect him, he waved off the crowd to face her alone. She had to grudgingly respect the fact that he moved his subordinates out of harm's way, but he was still her enemy.

With a final fortifying breath, Himeko charged. She fully expected someone to stop her as she crossed the fairly large open area between her and the royal, but the crowd just watched.

She was almost within striking distance and the Polaxian hadn't pulled a weapon to defend himself. She concluded he must be an expert in hand to hand combat. It didn't matter, she would dispatch him quickly and run for the exit she saw behind him.

"Himeko!"

Himeko stumbled with Daray's shout. She had to quickly divert the path of her *tessen* or she would strike the man she loved as he blocked her path to her enemy. She slammed into Daray, but her slight frame barely moved him as he wrapped his arms around her and buried his face in her hair.

"I thought I had lost you," Daray whispered into her hair. Himeko was shocked to feel tears drop onto her face. She looked up to find Daray crying. He cupped her cheeks in his hands and kissed her until she almost didn't remember her own name. "No more. From now on you are not to leave my sight. I don't think my heart can take anymore worry about the woman I love."

Himeko was stunned by Daray's admission. She never would have suspected that Daray returned the feeling that she kept hidden for the last couple of years. He had always been a perfect gentleman to her, but he had always remained reserved and aloof.

She almost forgot that they were surrounded by enemies until the shadow of the royal Polaxian fell across them. Himeko struck out with her war fan to defend Daray, only to have that same man stay her hand.

She looked up at Daray through narrowed

eyes.

"Give us a chance to explain. Things aren't what they seem here." Daray pushed her arm down beside her. She allowed him to, but she refused to give up her weapon.

The Polaxian shrugged like it didn't matter to him and smiled. "Why don't I let you freshen up and your friends can explain a few things. I hope to see you at dinner later."

With that he turned his back on Himeko and Daray and walked away. Most of the crowd followed his lead, leaving Himeko and Daray almost alone in what she could now see was a hangar of some sort. Several pods like the one she had been transported in surrounded the outside of the large space. Himeko looked above and gasped when she saw a clear barrier that gave her a view into the darkened waters they were below. She could make out the shadows of strange sea creatures as they passed by. Some came close enough to see within the light of facility's illumination. She watched in wonder as a group of creatures that rivaled the whales back on Earth swam by overhead. She was actually in an underwater city.

Daray tugged at her and she turned to him.

"It can be a little overwhelming at first." He gave her a shy smile. "But the reasons why it is here will make sense after a few things are explained."

Himeko started to shiver as the adrenaline left her body. She was still standing in her dripping clothes. She also needed to dry out her war fan to ensure it would be in top working order. Phase guns or pulse blades might be more practical, but she felt safe with the familiar weight of her *tessen*.

Daray noticed her shiver and shrugged out of his shirt to drape it around her shoulders. Himeko couldn't help the deep breath she took as his warmth surrounded her. The shirt smelled like him. She wasn't going to complain about the view either. Shirtless Daray was hot.

Daray was more lithe than the typical Vukasin. But his leaner physique was still very muscular and defined. Daray's training favored more elegant martial arts. He was a master sword dancer, his graceful form well suited to the art. Himeko had watched him practice his forms several times. Even now as he walked in front of her she had to resist the urge to reach out and run her hands down his rippling muscles.

She was so preoccupied with the beauty of

the man in front of her that she nearly ran into his back when he stopped in front of a door. Himeko blinked and looked around and blushed as she realized she couldn't remember how they arrived here.

Daray laid his hand on the pad near the door and it opened with a whoosh.

"We will have to program your DNA into the lock, so you can open the door later," Daray said as he entered a small but well-appointed space.

Himeko followed him into an area she recognized as personal quarters. At first she assumed that she was being assigned a space to sleep until something Daray said registered.

"…to keep us together I told Alaric that you were my mate."

"Mate?" Himeko's voice broke on the word.

Daray blushed and nodded. He refused to look Himeko in the eyes. "It was the most expedient way to make certain we wouldn't be separated." He looked around the room and sighed. "I'm afraid there is only one bed since they assumed we would share. I can use the floor while we are here. I don't mind."

He bustled around the room and pulled clean clothes from a compartment in the wall. He showed her where the bathroom was and babbled as he flitted around the room. Himeko found it adorable that he was nervous at the idea of sharing quarters with her. She couldn't help the giggle that left her lips.

"…I'm afraid the clothes are going to be a bit big. There isn't anyone in the base that is as delicate as you are."

She smiled at him as she took the clothes from his hands. She raised up and kissed his cheek. His voice trailed off as she turned and walked into the washroom.

During a blissfully warm shower, Himeko decided that fate had presented this opportunity and she wasn't going to lose it. Daray had already admitted that he loved her. He claimed her as mate in front of others. True, that was probably a tactical move, but Himeko was determined that she would be his mate in truth before they left this place. No more would she be the reserved proper maiden. Life was short and it was time to be brave enough to grasp what she really wanted, especially since it seemed that he wanted her too.

Himeko rinsed her hair and smiled as the

warm water caressed her body. She didn't have much experience in seduction, but she was a fast learner. Already, a plan was forming in her mind.

CHAPTER THIRTEEN

Daray groaned as he thought about Himeko in the other room naked with water cascading over her body. He vowed that he wouldn't dishonor her, but his libido had different ideas.

Daray sank down on the bed. Even before Himeko had disappeared, Daray had been researching the mating customs of the Earth women. Megan had introduced something they called a "marriage" ceremony. From what he could gather, the ceremony should come before the mating. That hadn't happened with Megan and Reijo. Curiosity had Daray wanting to ask Megan if that fact made her feel dishonored or if the fact that she already had a mate that she lost in the past changed how she viewed the "marriage." Daray had learned enough about Himeko's past to know that she never had a mate and Daray didn't want to mess up their future "marriage" by being a beast who thought only of satisfaction. But his need for her was riding him hard.

Daray lay back on the bed and covered his face with his arm. He heaved a large sigh. He was an honorable man. He was in control of his body and mind. Daray repeated the mantra that normally calmed and cleared his mind. It wasn't working so well tonight. He couldn't clear his mind of images of her. He punched the bed in frustration.

"Are you all right?"

Himeko's voice startled him and he sat up abruptly. His eyes widened. She stood in the doorway between the washroom and the main living space only wearing the drying cloth wrapped around her.

Daray swallowed and stammered, "F…fine…I'm fine."

She walked towards him. He watched her delicate body undulate in that hypnotizing way that only females seemed to be able to move. He nearly had to sit on his hands to keep from reaching out for her. Where was the cool control he was known for when he needed it?

She stopped right in front of him. With him sitting on the bed and her standing they were almost eye level with each other. It would take nothing for Daray to lean forward and kiss Himeko, something he had been dreaming about since Ghaleb had placed her in his home. His want had turned to need as Daray learned more about the woman. She earned his respect and slowly stole his heart.

Daray brought himself back to the moment at hand only to discover that his body had been leaning in for a kiss without him even knowing it. But Daray knew that once started he wouldn't be able to stop with a kiss and he had vowed that he wouldn't mate Himeko until they were able to have the ceremony of marriage. He would never let her feel that he dishonored her in any way, and he wanted her to know that he respected her human culture as well.

Himeko had closed her eyes and leaned towards Daray in preparation of a kiss. Instead Daray pushed her away and abruptly stood up. He snatched his hands away as if she burned his skin. He almost turned her to examine the colorful design he discovered on her back as he walked past, but he knew if he touched her again that he wouldn't stop touching her.

"I'm going to speak with Alaric." He waved a hand in Himeko's general direction. "It will give you time to dress." He marched stiffly toward the door of their quarters. "I will return shortly to take you to get food."

Daray left abruptly. He leaned his forehead against the closed door. He was trying to preserve Himeko's honor, yet he couldn't mistake the hurt look in her eyes when he set her away from him. That look more than the distance cooled his ardor. It seemed like all he did was take missteps with Himeko. Hopefully he wouldn't hurt her so bad that she wouldn't forgive him once their marriage was complete.

*****

Himeko stood in their quarters trying not to cry. What had she done wrong? She had been so certain that Daray was going to kiss her, but he had run away instead. He had said that he loved her. Had he only said that in the heat of the moment? Was she misconstruing what kind of love he had for her? She didn't know.

She had no idea what she was doing trying to

seduce Daray. Seduction was not skill she was accomplished at. Because of who her father was, she had very few men willing to attempt a relationship with her. The one other sexual partner she had in her life had come on to her. At the time, she was flattered until she discovered that her 'boyfriend' was just using her to gain access to her father.

Maybe she was misreading Daray. She had her own lack of experience and then there were the cultural differences between her world and his. It was possible that there was a different meaning that she didn't understand to his actions.

Himeko's rational mind was trying to convince her that although Daray obviously cared for her, he didn't return her feelings. Himeko's heart reminded her of the look of lust that flared in his eyes and the rather obvious reaction of the male parts of his anatomy.

Himeko smiled at the thought that she was the one to cause those reactions. It also meant that she could affect Daray in the same way he affected her. It was too early in the game to give up. This would be a challenge that Himeko won.

She hadn't reached for much for herself in this life. She was reaching for Daray. She wanted him and she was fairly certain that he wanted her too. She just needed to convince him that they belonged together.

CHAPTER FOURTEEN

Alaric waved Daray over when the Vukasin entered the common eating area. Daray wasn't quite sure what to make of the Polaxian. Alaric had won over Raylan, but Daray hadn't spent enough time with the man to form his own opinion.

Daray knew that Alaric wanted something from him and Himeko. The question was what.

"Your beautiful mate is returned, despite the attack of a pod of the giant dalli fish; yet you look miserable." Alaric clapped him on the back as Daray took a seat next to him.

Daray wasn't about to speak with a virtual stranger in regards to his love life, so instead he used his political skill to deflect his true feelings.

"Yes, she is alive. I am grateful to the universe for that." Daray looked into Alaric's eyes with an intense stare. "But we are still in enemy territory."

Alaric shook his head. "You are among friends, not enemies, Daray of the Nardo."

Daray gave his politician's smile, "That remains to be seen, Alaric. You know as well as I do that you are hoping to gain something from us. The question is just what it is you want."

Alaric turned towards the entrance of the common area and Daray just knew that his attention was drawn by Himeko. It amazed Daray that the woman seemed oblivious of her effect on the males that surrounded her. Five hells, half of the Nardo clan was in love with her. It made him wonder what he could possibly offer her that she couldn't find with someone else.

Daray's dark thoughts reflected in his face as he turned to watch her come to him. He saw her smile falter when she saw his scowl. She quickly hid her hurt behind the serene mask she normally wore, but Daray had seen it. He mentally kicked himself for hurting her once again. Maybe she would be better off with another man that didn't seem to hurt her feelings at every turn. But the beast within him growled at the thought of her with someone else. Every cell in his body screamed that she was his.

"Lady Himeko," Alaric beamed. "I find it amazing that someone as delicate and beautiful as you could have such ruthless skill in battle."

Daray noticed that Himeko unconsciously touched the war fan that she had tucked into her belt.

Himeko sat across from Alaric and inclined her head, "When you grow up with a father such as mine, you find such skills useful."

Daray's ears perked up at that confession. Himeko had rarely spoken of her childhood. Daray was quickly realizing that perhaps he didn't know the woman quite as well as he had thought. He didn't doubt that he knew her character and the woman she was now. It was the things in her life that shaped her into the woman she was that he didn't really know. He found that he wanted to learn those things about her. Who was he kidding? He wanted to know everything about her.

In Himeko's typical soft, calm voice, she

asked, "So am I a bauble to be fought over by the royal family?"

"What makes you think I am a royal?" Alaric asked.

Himeko just raised a delicate brow at him and Alaric just laughed.

"You know most people outside of Polax don't even recognize the fact that the royal bloodline has a distinctive physical feature."

Himeko shrugged as she reached for a bit of bread that was in a basket in the middle of the table. "I have had the unique experience of being an alien that has had the privilege of dealing with several Polaxian royals. One would be a fool not to notice that only the royals had black tips to their hair. Though I suppose it is possible that it was a fashion statement rather than natural."

Alaric ran his hand through his mane of hair. "No, it is natural. Cubs are tested at an early age to make sure it is natural. It is a death sentence for anyone to try and fake the look."

Daray interrupted. "If you are a member of the royal family, why are you hiding?"

Alaric sighed, "Polax keeps its internal politics to itself, but suffice it to say that the royal family is not as solidly in control as they would have you believe. Times are changing and there are many Polaxians that are tired of the caste system that keeps them confined and the xenophobic policies that make sure the rest of the galaxy hates them."

Himeko quietly regarded Alaric with her dark, soulful eyes. Even without saying a word, she could prompt someone into speaking more than they intended. Alaric proved no different.

"The royal family ruling now wasn't always in power. My grandfather was once king of the Polaxians. He was a rather progressive man. He had a vision for the planet that eliminated the caste system and with it the slavery that has become so entrenched in the Polaxian culture."

"I would have thought that those who led the coup would have killed off your line to make sure they kept power." Himeko spoke behind her lifted hand as she just finished chewing and swallowing a piece of bread. Daray found the way she ate so daintily adorable.

"They tried. My father was murdered along with my older brother. I was a small child when the takeover occurred. My mother wasn't my father's legal wife. My mother was from a lower caste, but the royal genetics showed true in me."

Daray leaned forward, "So you have a vested interest in destroying the caste system."

Alaric shrugged, "You know as well as I do everyone has an ulterior motive to their actions. Very few are saintly enough to be truly altruistic. The question is whether they are honest about it or not."

"You need us for something." Himeko tilted her head to the side. "I think it is time you tell about what that something is."

*****

Himeko studied the Polaxian called Alaric. She could see the family resemblance between him and Listar, but Alaric lacked a certain cruelty around his eyes that the reigning royal family seemed to have. She looked around at the various people milling about. She saw several species who she assumed were slaves that disappeared much in the way Raylan had. The difference between here and the surface was the Polaxians in the group.

On the surface, the Polaxians would have

treated other species as if they were somehow less simply because they weren't born a Polaxian. Here they treated those of different species with respect as an equal. She even saw a few Polaxians who were obviously a couple with an alien species.

Himeko had to admit that she was seeing the values and society that Alaric claimed his grandfather had tried to create. However, she wasn't naïve enough to believe that this small group shared the opinion of the majority.

Alaric watched the pair, and the Vukasin stared right back. He had done his research and knew that Daray was an important clan leader. He also know that the delicate woman next to him was not originally from Vukas, though the Vukasins, both the rebel Tanis and the main home world government, seemed to be the only ones who knew of her species' location.

The female called Himeko fascinated Alaric. She was so delicate, but obviously warrior trained. Yet, she most often presented the patient and calm exterior of a saint. She rose into a position of power on an alien world, from captive to diplomat. He heard Raylan and Daray both refer to her as their princess, giving her a title of royalty without the benefit of birth or mating. She would make someone an amazing queen with that regal fire and calm façade.

Daray frowned at Alaric as if reading his mind. Alaric sighed and forced himself to remember that she already had a mate.

"The simple answer is I want to create what we have here on the surface." Alaric leaned back in his chair. One arm draped across the back of the chair while his other hand thoughtfully stroked the hair of his mane. "Polax needs to change. This continued raiding and enslaving of other species is rapidly building animosity. Those worlds that have outlawed slavery are no longer willing to treaty or trade with this world. As much as the current rulers want to hide the fact, we are running out of resources. My grandfather saw the beginnings of this, and it was one of the main reasons he tried to abolish the slave system. While my grandfather's reasons were more practical than altruistic, mine are not."

Himeko regarded the exiled royal. "You were raised in hiding here among the escaped slaves."

She had made it a statement rather than asking a question, but Alaric nodded in response.

"What is this place?" Daray asked.

"It is a forgotten military science facility. At one point there were numerous researchers here studying the oceans. There are actually several of these facilities dotted around the home world. But before my grandfather took the throne, this study was defunded and the facilities abandoned. It didn't take long for most Polaxians to forget about these places, but the slaves didn't."

Himeko tilted her head and narrowed her eyes. "There had to be records of this place…expense reports, building schematics. How is it possible that the royal family doesn't know?"

Alaric smiled and gave a small laugh, "I wondered the same myself as I got older, but when I took over as the leader here, I learned that the slaves had infiltrated various facilities and systematically destroyed any mention of the underwater cities. They are also the ones who started the rumors about sea monsters that snatched people from the beaches."

"So those who went missing at the beaches wouldn't be searched for," Daray said.

"Exactly."

Himeko leveled a look on Alaric. "While I

admire the changes you want to bring to your world, you and I both know it isn't as simple as you state. What are you wanting from us?"

"An alliance."

Himeko nodded. "I thought as much. You realize that you are asking my people to step into what would amount to a civil war."

"Your people are already involved. The Tanis clan has an alliance with the current regime," Alaric pointed out.

"But we aren't traitors," Daray interjected.

"And as such, we do not have the power to make the decisions you are asking of us," Himeko added.

"But you have the power to give me access to those that can make those decisions."

Himeko nodded at Alaric. Between her and Daray's connections to the Nardo as well as Megan and Ghaleb, they did have the power to connect Alaric to the highest echelons of the Vukasin government.

"You can't expect our people to get involved

in what will be a bloody conflict for nothing. What can you offer in exchange?" Himeko's voice was still the soft spoken voice Daray was used to, but now there was an iron edge to it. He was beginning to understand why she was one of their best diplomats. She wasn't flashy. She carried herself with a quiet elegance. But she had a knack for presenting herself and her points in a way that revealed the strength beneath the serene.

Himeko crossed her arms and stared down the much larger Polaxian.

"I appreciate what you are trying to do, Alaric, and I think it is a worthy cause. But I cannot advocate getting involved in your conflict without something more than the Tanis already being involved. Our government is pursuing the Tanis issue outside of Polax. You have to give me something more than that."

Alaric pushed away from the table and abruptly stood. "Fair enough. If you would come with me, there is something I think you should see."

Himeko and Daray exchanged looks but rose to follow Alaric.

CHAPTER FIFTEEN

Himeko jogged to keep up with the longer legs of Daray and Alaric. She refused to complain though; by the time they wove their way through the fourth block of apartments, she was ready to throw something at the back of their heads.

Himeko was so glad when Alaric stopped at a cross section. She had to take a few deep breaths to slow her heartbeat. Just walking with a pair of men shouldn't be this much of a work out.

"Why did we stop?" Daray asked as Alaric looked around.

Alaric didn't answer him. He decided to continue down the left-hand corridor. Himeko observed the area as they passed through. She decided to continue at her normal stride so she could actually see more than a blur of her surroundings. Soon the men were well ahead of her, but she still had them in her line of sight.

Himeko was surprised to see numerous women with several children. All of the children seemed to be hybrids; many obviously had some Polaxian parentage. Himeko looked around; besides her escort, there didn't seem to be any males in the section who weren't children.

Himeko turned her head as she heard a woman gasp. There was a Ludian woman standing there with her jeweled eyes opened wide with fright at the sight of the men. Himeko really looked at the women she passed. All of them kept an eye on the passing males. Some had looks of wary respect while others had the same terrified look as the first woman from Ludus Prime.

It didn't take long for Himeko to figure out that this area housed female former slaves. Without even asking, Himeko knew that all of these women shared traumatic experiences of sexual assault and rape.

The men turned a corner and Himeko jogged

to catch up. She saw several more Ludus Prime women. She wondered if Alaric would allow her to contact Zamira and Akia to let them know that some of their people were here. Her curiosity was peaked. Was Alaric showing them this sector of the underwater city to gain sympathy for his cause?

Alaric and Daray stood in front of a door. Daray was looking around. His face visibly relaxed when he spotted Himeko heading towards them.

Daray wrapped an arm around Himeko's shoulder and gave it a gentle squeeze when she walked up beside him. As she leaned into his touch, he dropped his arm. She looked up at him. His face was flushed and he wouldn't look her in the eye.

"I was afraid we had lost you," Daray said, staring straight ahead.

Himeko's normal serene façade fell a bit. She was tired of these hot and cold signals from the man standing beside her.

"Well, my legs happen to be a lot shorter than yours," she bit at him.

Daray hung his head and Himeko almost instantly regretted her angry tone. She sighed. The two of them needed to figure out what was between them otherwise they were going to drive each other apart. Himeko knew that she needed more than just the respectful friendship that they had up until now. At one point she had thought that just having the man she loved in her life would be enough. But recent events forced her to be honest with herself. She needed more or she needed to move on.

She wanted the more but she wasn't sure of what Daray wanted. There were times she thought he wanted the same but when she tried to get closer he pushed her away. It was damn confusing,.

Alaric pressed the intercom and waited. It didn't take long before a sweet feminine voice filtered out the speaker.

"Yes? Who is it?"

"Brandy, it's Alaric. There are some people I think you should meet."

The speaker went silent. For a moment Himeko wondered if the woman behind the door was going to open it. If she was as traumatized as the other women in this sector, it was possible that she may not. Seeing the two huge men on the view screen would give any woman pause. Himeko pushed her way in front of the men. Perhaps another woman present would make the person on the other side of the door more comfortable.

It took a few more moments, but the door slid open a crack. Himeko saw a pair of wide blue eyes staring back at her. The woman regarded Himeko with interest. Then their eyes met and Himeko saw the mystery woman's eyes widen.

"You're human, aren't you?"

The door opened enough that Himeko could now see clearly that the woman standing before her was human. Daray had said that there were a few human women who had been up for sale at the slave auction, but Himeko doubted that Alaric would make a point of introducing them to just another human. After all, the same impact could have been accomplished with a woman from Ludus Prime since Vukas and that planet were now so tightly tied together

So what was it a bout this woman that made her special? Himeko could see a sprinkling of freckles across pale skin. She had long, thick chestnut hair. The woman wasn't much taller than Himeko, though she boasted a set of lush curves. Back on Earth she would have been considered overweight, but she was well proportioned.

"Yes, I am human," Himeko replied.

The woman nodded. "At first I thought Alaric might have brought another woman from Ludus Prime, but your eyes are dark, not the jewel-like eyes that they have."

"I'm Himeko Tsubaki, formerly from Japan."

The woman gave Himeko a smile that lit up her whole face. In that moment, the woman transformed into a great beauty.

"I'm Brandy Smith formerly from Oklahoma."

"Brandy, may we come in? There is something we need to discuss." Brandy's eyes shot to Alaric. She had almost forgotten the men were there in her excitement of seeing another human.

Himeko turned to Daray and Alaric. She didn't know Alaric well enough to read him yet, but she knew that Daray could sense the woman's discomfort in the males' presence.

"M'lady, I can remain out here if it would make you more comfortable," Daray offered.

Brandy sighed and ran a hand through her

thick hair. "No, that's all right. Come in." She moved aside to allow the three into her sanctuary.

As he passed, Daray turned to Brandy. His kind face softened and he asked once more, "Are you sure?"

That gentle regard for others was one of the reasons that Himeko loved Daray so much. It didn't matter if it inconvenienced him or made his task more difficult, he instinctually knew when a person was fragile or frightened and he would go out of his way to make them as comfortable as possible.

Brandy gave Daray a slight smile, "Yes, come in." She gestured for him to enter her home. "Besides, having you hang around outside would make the other women nervous."

Himeko and the men entered a neat little apartment. It was a little larger than the quarters they had been given, but it was obvious that Brandy had been living there for quite a while. There were comfortable crocheted throws on the couch. Himeko spotted a basket filled with yarn and surmised that Brandy had created them herself. Little potted plants dotted the room, softening the utilitarian look. All in all Brandy had created a cozy retreat in a harsh environment.

"You will need to make this quick, Alaric," Brandy said as she sat in a chair across from her visitors. "You know that the educators will release the school age children for lunch soon. I will be busy then."

"I'm sorry, Brandy. But we will remain."

Brandy's eyes flashed, and despite her obvious discomfort around large males, she stood and advanced on Alaric.

"No," Brandy said through clenched teeth.

"It's for the good of everyone," Alaric sighed.

Brandy snorted and clenched her fists. "Everyone? You mean it is good for you! You didn't even speak to me first to find out if this is what I want."

"Things have changed, Brandy." Alaric leaned forward and took Brandy's clenched fist in his hand. "I promise I wouldn't do this if I didn't think it was necessary."

Himeko and Daray watched the interplay. She was mentally calculating with the scant clues she had garnered. She had her suspicions but she needed more information.

"Damn it." Brandy turned from Alaric, pulling her hand from his. She started banging around in the small kitchen area preparing drinks for the guests forced on her. "I'm tired of being a pawn in other people's games, Alaric."

"I can assure you this is no game."

Brandy leveled a look on Alaric that made the man shrink away. Himeko almost chuckled; it was the look that every mother learned to give an unruly child. As Alaric fell into silence, Brandy returned to preparing something to drink and cleaning her already neat kitchen along the way.

Himeko could see that Brandy was a domestic woman. She was the kind of woman who turned to cooking or cleaning when she needed to feel more in control on the situation around her. It was a skill that in many ways Himeko lacked. Himeko's mother, what little she could remember of her before her death, was a lot like that. She brought a feeling of home no matter how difficult a situation was. Himeko watched that same skill in Brandy and for a moment was envious of the woman's natural maternal nature.

She looked over and saw Daray watching Brandy with open curiosity. Himeko wondered if she were more domestic if Daray would quit pulling away from her. Wondering 'what if' was useless. Himeko was Himeko, and nothing would change that. Daray either loved her as she was or she needed to move on to someone who would.

Brandy set glasses filled with a fruit juice of some sort in front of her guests. Himeko was just about to ask her about her experiences when the apartment's door slid open.

The door framed a child who looked to be about seven years of age.

"Mom, I'm home," the boy bellowed before stopping short upon seeing a house full of people.

He had his mother's blue eyes, but immediately Himeko could see why Alaric wanted them to meet this family now. Himeko heard Daray suck in a breath and she knew that he saw it as well.

Brandy beckoned her son to come to her and she wrapped a protective arm around her child. The child could have walked out of the paintings of a young Ghaleb. Himeko knew that a genetic test would be needed for confirmation, but she was fairly certain that this child was an Ivalio.

This changed everything, and the smile that Himeko saw on Alaric's face when she turned to him told her that he had known it would all along.

"This is my son, Alexander Smith." Brandy emphasized the surname. "Say hello to our guests, Alex."

"Hello," the boy said quietly as he placed himself between his mother and the men in the room.

Himeko smiled. Even at a young age the child was trying to protect his mother. He would grow up to be an honorable man with instincts like that. Though looking at the hand Brandy placed on his shoulder, Himeko was certain the woman wouldn't allow him to grow up to be anything but honorable.

"Daray, would you take Alaric and leave?" Himeko asked quietly.

"Huh?"

"Brandy and I need to talk, and I think it would be better if you men weren't here when that occurred."

Daray frowned slightly, but he knew he could trust Himeko's judgement. In the end he stood, thanking Brandy for her hospitality. Alaric protested, but a quelling look from both women had him scurrying from the apartment as well.

"Alex, honey, would you go to your room to eat your lunch and do your homework?"

"I can eat in my room?" Alex asked in wonder. At Brandy's nod, he ran to the kitchen to snatch up the plate of food that had been prepared and disappeared into the other room.

Himeko chuckled. "He's not normally allowed to eat in his bedroom is he?"

Brandy gave a sad smile. "It won't take him long to finish, so let's talk."

CHAPTER SIXTEEN

Himeko sipped her juice and just remained silent. This was Brandy's story to tell. Himeko knew the woman was smart enough to figure out what she wanted to know. You didn't survive what Brandy had survived without being an intelligent woman. Himeko should know; she survived something similar. But unlike Brandy, she had a support system in Megan and the other women. Brandy suffered on her own without even the benefit of a friend. In many ways it could be argued that Brandy was the stronger of the two women.

"I saw your face when Alex came in. You know whose son he is don't you?" Brandy set her cup aside with a sigh.

"I have my suspicions, but only a genetic test would confirm it. I'm assuming that Alaric knows?" Himeko took another sip of her drink, "This is really delicious...I don't think I have had this particular fruit before, though it tastes somewhat familiar."

"That's because it is a hybrid that I created. It crosses the daoma fruit from here on Polax with the paya-paya from Vukas. Both are similar to citrus fruits that we had back on Earth. The daomo is sweeter but difficult to grow here in planting beds. The tree just gets too large. The paya-paya grows more bushy and produces more juice. A few generations of crosses isolating the features I want and there you have it." Brandy's face lit up when she talked about her work with the plants.

"That's rather brilliant," Himeko said as she drank more of the juice.

Brandy waved her off. "I grew up a farm girl. So that sort of thing is second nature to me."

Himeko reached over and laid her hand on Brandy's. She gave a gentle squeeze. "Don't ever sell your accomplishments short, Brandy. It might have been second nature on Earth, but you found yourself on an alien world. Not only did you survive, but it seems to me that you are thriving. Not every woman would be able to say the same thing."

Brandy gave a sad smile. "I might be surviving, but somehow I still find myself controlled by others."

"I won't make excuses for what Alaric has done, but I can understand it." Himeko set her cup aside. "Leaders have to make decisions that are for the good of the majority, and sometimes that means disregarding the minority."

Brandy was thoughtful for a moment and then sighed. "I know…and honestly I can't blame him. Our population is reaching unsustainable levels in the ocean cities. Some of the others are worse than here…rationing food and water. If he doesn't find a way to expand to the surface, a lot of people are going to die."

Himeko gave a sad smile. "But it doesn't make him breaking a confidence hurt any less, does it?"

"No, it doesn't."

"You know I am going to have to tell the Vukasin Imperial Council about Alex."

"I wish you wouldn't…."

"You know there are other half-human children on Vukas now as well. And many of the woman have found happiness there."

"Have you?"

"I'm working on it."

Brandy tilted her head and studied Himeko. "You really like being on Vukas?"

"On Earth, I was just a woman no matter how hard I trained or how much I accomplished. In fact, I was taken because I had run off to be alone because my father had arranged my marriage because as a female I wasn't good enough to run the organization. I wasn't brutal enough or hard enough."

Brandy picked up her glass and took a sip. She gave a small laugh, "You make it sound like you grew up in the mob."

Himeko leveled a look on her.

"Oh my god…seriously?" Brandy exclaimed.

"The yakuza have a little more legitimacy than the Italian mob in my home country, but yes they are very similar."

"So why is Vukas better? Females were property from my short time there." Brandy's eyes shadowed, and for a moment Himeko wondered just what she had experienced, but she wasn't going to pry into something that was obviously painful."

"In the beginning, it wasn't. But they made a tactical error when they took Megan and her daughter Abby. That woman is a force of nature." Himeko chuckled. "And now she is in a position of power by their own laws and customs. In fact, she could take control of the entire planet if she really wanted to."

"But she doesn't want to?"

Himeko shook her head. "She just wants to take care of her family. She fell in love with the commander over all of the armed forces on the planet. But she keeps the threat of takeover to use as leverage to protect the women on the planet. It's not perfect, but so far it seems to be a good balance."

"And what is your role on Vukas?"

"I'm a diplomat. I am helping them break away from their xenophobic policies as we try to find and destroy the Tanis traitors."

Brandy traced lines in the condensation on

her glass. "You know that the royal family is heavily tied to the Tanis. They have been their primary slavers for years. It was how I ended up here a few years ago."

"I'm surprised that the Tanis would relinquish Alex. If they managed to kill off Ghaleb then they could possibly take over the government on Vukas with him."

"They didn't let him go. I stole him back with Alaric's help. The Tanis are still looking for us."

CHAPTER SEVENTEEN

"Daray, I fully understand why she doesn't want Ghaleb to know about Alex." Himeko sank into the couch and leaned her head back. She had learned a lot from talking to Brandy without the men present, and now she was torn about what she should do.

"Himeko, that boy is the heir to the royal throne of the Vukasin Empire. You have to tell Ghaleb."

They had been going round and round for over an hour now. It was clear cut to Daray what they should do, but Himeko wasn't so sure it was the right thing.

"The empire isn't going to fall without Alex. But exposing them will put a huge target on their backs. They are safe right now."

Daray sat down next to Himeko and reached over to gently turn her head to look him in the eyes. "But for how long? You said yourself that Alaric showed his hand because he is desperate. What is going to happen when the supplies run out? They are going to be exposed at some point. At least on Vukas they would have the protection of the royal house."

Himeko wanted to quit discussing Brandy and what they should do. She gently closed her eyes and leaned towards Daray. She wanted to kiss the man. Maybe if she did she would know if they had a future or not.

Just as she could feel the heat from his skin, Daray abruptly jumped up. Himeko wanted to scream in frustration. It was becoming clear to her that she was probably mistaken that he desired her for something more than friendship. After all, his statement that she was the woman he loved could mean so many different things. His love for her could be along the lines of sister or friend instead of the intimate feelings she harbored for him.

Himeko had to blink back tears as Daray rushed to the other side of the room. She never knew that rejection could hurt so much. She refused to let him see her break down, so she stood up and marched to the door of their quarters.

"I'm going out for a while," Himeko declared.

"What? Why? You shouldn't go out on your own. I'll go with you."

"I would rather you didn't," she stated through clenched teeth. "Am I a prisoner? Do I need an escort?"

"No, of course not."

Daray looked genuinely confused, and it pissed Himeko off that her first reaction was to sooth him.

"Then I am going for a walk…alone."

Himeko rushed out the door, letting it slide shut behind her before she quickly took off. She had no idea where she was going, but it really didn't matter because she just knew that right now she couldn't be in the same room as Daray.

Himeko rushed through the crowds of people, turning down any corridor that seemed to have fewer bodies in it. Soon she found herself in what appeared to be a cargo storage area. It was blissfully quiet here. For the first time in a couple of years, she really missed Earth. She missed the quiet little shrine that had been her refuge when she needed to think. Even though it was the place of her abduction, she still thought of that place fondly. The little old monk who had taken care of the place treated her like a beloved granddaughter. He rarely had given her advice, but he listened as she worked through her own problems. She really wished she could talk to him again.

She sat on the ground next to one of the large containers. She drew up her knees and laid her head on them. She couldn't stop the tears this time.

That was how Raylan found her, sobbing alone in the dim room. She was so wrapped up in her broken heart that she hadn't even noticed him until he sat beside her and drew her into his arms.

Later, Himeko would be embarrassed about him finding her like that, but right now the comfort of another felt good. She sobbed on his shoulder as he held her tightly. All of the stress, all of the senseless lives lost, all of the rejection…all of it flowed out of her eyes and down her cheeks to soak Raylan's shirt.

When her sobs subsided, Raylan cupped her cheek and lifted her face to look at him. His thumb gently brushed away the last of her tears.

"Hey Princess, want to talk about it?"

"There's nothing you can do, Raylan." Himeko wiped her face and tried to straighten her hair.

"You know you don't always have to wear the mask," Raylan stated as he rubbed a hand up and down Himeko's back. The motion was soothing...not demanding or sexual in any way, just comforting.

Himeko sighed. Other than Megan she hadn't really formed any real friendships. She looked over at Raylan. She had been wary of every male she had met, even Daray at first, because they had all looked at her with varying degrees of lust or ownership. She had never felt that from Raylan.

"Why is it you are the only male that doesn't look at me with desire in your eyes?"

Raylan knew she was purposely changing the

subject, but he let her.

"Vain much?" His words would have been hurtful if he hadn't had a teasing smile on his face. "I would think that answer would be rather obvious."

Himeko still looked at him with confusion.

"I'm attracted to males, Princess."

Himeko's mouth formed a little 'O' as she realized what he was saying. She shouldn't be surprised. Earth had its fair share of homosexuals, so why wouldn't other planets? Especially a planet who had so few women to begin with.

"Does that bother you?" Himeko could see the vulnerability in Raylan's eyes. It would appear that those that were different faced similar issues no matter the planet.

"No. It just surprises me is all." She leaned against his shoulder as he wrapped an arm around her shoulder. "In fact, it is kind of nice not wondering if I am accidently encouraging interest or flirting when I didn't mean to."

"So tell me what is really going on."

Himeko sighed. "Have you ever fallen for

somebody but they don't feel the same about you?" Raylan just gave her a look and she laughed softly. "Point taken."

"Would this happen to involve a certain dour clan leader? You know he's crazy about you."

Himeko shook her head and blinked back the tears that threatened again. "No, he's not."

"I see the way he looks at you when he thinks no one else is watching."

"It doesn't matter; he has already rejected me."

Raylan frowned. "What do you mean?"

"I tried to seduce him. I've only kissed him once because I caught him by surprise in the heat of the moment. Every time since he pushes me away." Himeko sighed. "He doesn't want me, Raylan."

"That *frexing* idiot. I'm going to kill him."

CHAPTER EIGHTEEN

Daray paced the length of their quarters. He couldn't mistake the flash of hurt in Himeko eyes. He knew she left because she was angry. He didn't understand her reaction at all. He was trying to do the honorable thing.

If she had been Vukasin, he would have just taken her and given her the mating bite to seal them both together for the rest of their lives. But she wasn't Vukasin; she was human from Earth. He had spent countless hours studying the customs and rituals of mating on Earth. He knew that some had casual sex. It was all over the media files and history that the Vukasins had downloaded on their various trips to acquire breeding-compatible females. Those encounters seemed transient, going from intimate partner to intimate partner. Daray didn't want something temporary. Then he read about the marriage ceremony where humans vowed to be together 'until death do us part.' That was what he wanted, so he spent countless hours poring over the ceremony, and most religions that he could find stated that sex should not occur until after the marriage ceremony took place.

Daray was learning that such a sanction was probably the greatest test of strength and will that he had ever undertook. He had often wondered in the last few days since finding Himeko again if this test was what created the bond between those who participated in the marriage ceremony.

He wondered if he was performing the parts of that ritual correctly. He could honestly say that Himeko seemed to be drawn to him in ways he had not seen in their past, but this ritual seemed to be causing her emotional pain. He didn't want to cause her pain, especially when he was just trying to be an honorable man worthy of her. Maybe he could convince her that a blending of Vukasin and human mating would be best.

Resolved to do just that, Daray went in search of Himeko. He couldn't find her in any of the common areas and he didn't run across her in the corridors. After a while he had to admit that walking around such a large complex was inefficient. So he went in search of Alaric.

Daray found the Polaxian directing the off-loading of supplies. For as large a complex and the sheer number of people that Daray observed, the amount of supplies seemed woefully inadequate.

"Alaric!" Daray called.

The hulking leader turned and waved Daray over. Alaric clapped him on the back and smiled.

"Daray, my friend. Have you come to tell me that your lady-mate has decided to look on my request favorably?"

"I'm afraid that is not why I am here."

Alaric frowned and examined Daray's face. Daray had his normal stoic mask in place, but there was something in his eyes: a strain of worry that wasn't there before.

Alaric motioned Daray away from the crowd. They moved towards a quiet alcove. Alaric took the data pad from one of his workers and told him they were free to go once the supplies were stowed away.

"Your supply shipment seems a little on the lean side," Daray said.

Alaric shrugged and sat across from Daray, "I'm sure that the state of our supply stores isn't why you are here."

Daray ran a hand through his usually neat hair, leaving it sticking up in messy spikes. It was a telling sign about Daray's state of agitation. Alaric waited. He had a feeling that if he pressed Daray he would close himself off.

Eventually Daray sighed and Alaric knew his patience would be rewarded.

"Himeko and I had a disagreement."

Alaric smiled. "Is that all? It is not unusual for mates to fight." Alaric leaned forward and waggled his brows at Alaric. "I'm told that some even fight just so they can make up."

Daray ducked his head with a slight blush. Alaric had wondered at the almost innocence of feeling he witnessed between the Vukasin clan leader and the little human woman.

"So what is the problem?" Alaric sifted through the information on the data pad as he waited for Daray's response.

"She left our quarters and now I can't find her," Daray admitted.

That had Alaric stopping his work. The underwater city was fairly safe, but there was always a chance that their enemies had infiltrated. It was one of the reasons that Alaric had made sure the tracking programs were always in working order.

Alaric turned to the computer console on the far wall and entered his authorization code. "Computer, locate Ambassador Himeko."

"The ambassador is located in cargo storage area three." The computer displayed a map with a flashing blip indicating where Himeko was located.

"Do you want me to go with you?" Alaric asked.

Daray stood and shook his head. He didn't want Alaric to find out that they weren't mates in truth "No. This is something that Himeko and I need to resolve."

"As you wish." Alaric stood. "I need to finish my work here anyway."

Daray followed the twisting corridors until here reached the outer edges of the underwater city. It was no wonder why he hadn't found Himeko. This storage area was well off the beaten path. Himeko obviously wanted to be alone.

Daray hesitated. Should he disturb her? She had obviously been distraught when she left their quarters. Though, if he was honest with himself, he didn't understand why. He had almost initiated intimate contact that would have led to him mating with her. But he was able to get himself back under control so as to not dishonor her. Could she be angry at seeing his weakness around her? Navigating human mating rituals was proving more difficult than he had first thought. Maybe he should talk to Megan to figure out where he was going wrong.

His footsteps echoed in the empty hallway, and the shadows deepened as he moved further away from the crowds of people who made up the residents of the complex. Daray's mind was filled with thoughts of how to navigate his courting of Himeko. He had never made a move without careful deliberation, and he approached mating with the same methodical planning that he did everything else. Why did he seem to keep having missteps?

Daray turned the corner and opened the doors to the large storage area the computer claimed Himeko was in. He looked around and didn't see her at first. Then a flash of movement drew his eyes to the other side of the large room. Sitting next to a large storage container he saw the cascade of Himeko's long black hair. It took a moment for what he was seeing to register.

Himeko was there, just as the computer said she would be; however, she wasn't alone. Daray had the air sucked from his lungs as he saw Himeko in the arms of another male. His reaction was immediate and visceral. She was his! She belonged in his arms, not someone else's.

All thoughts of his carefully planned courtship disappeared as his beast rose to the surface. Daray rarely phased outside of training; he had too much control for that. But the sight of his woman in another's arms traded his tight control for primal rage.

Daray howled, startling the couple. The pair stood and the male, who he could now see was Raylan, shoved Himeko behind him to protect her. The move enraged Daray even more. Himeko was his to protect, his to love…no one else.

Raylan phased to face the charging Daray. The two men clashed in a whirlwind of fur and claws. It was a fearsome reminder that underneath Daray's calm exterior lay a predatory warrior.

Himeko watched in horrified fascination at Daray's loss of his tight control. She knew that she had to get the two men to stop before one of them killed the other, but she still took perverse pleasure in the thought that Daray may have lost control because of her. It would serve the big idiot right if that was the case.

Himeko picked up a tool and hurled it at the back of Daray's head. If he had been human, it probably would have knocked him out. In his phased stated it just annoyed him enough to turn to Himeko with a snarl.

"*Aho! Baka!* Stupid idiot!"

Tears flowed down Himeko's face as she yelled at Daray. All of her frustration and confusion broke through her usually serene façade. She picked up any loose item she could get her hands on and threw them at Daray.

As soon as Daray released him, Raylan

moved away with a panting chuckle in his phased form. He shook his head and returned to his regular appearance. He had thought that Daray needed his ass kicked to get the message through his thick logical head. It seemed that Himeko had that well in hand, and Raylan was not needed for the moment. He quickly left the storage area. Rylan would check on the pair later. Hopefully they would sort their feelings out between each other.

Daray shifted out of his phased form as he dodged the missiles Himeko continued to hurtle at him. He didn't understand her anger. She was the one who was in another's arms. He should be angry, not her.

Daray was done with trying to do things the human way. Himeko needed to know she belonged to him. She was his mate. His! No other's.

That thought had Daray pulling himself up to his full impressive height. He saw Himeko falter at his change in demeanor, but then the anger won out again as she continued to berate him. Daray stalked towards her, deflecting each item launched at him.

Himeko shifted her stance as he neared. When he reached for her, she used her training to keep his hands from grabbing her. It was a primal fight for dominance, a mating dance as old as the stars.

Daray gave a feral grin as he matched Himeko blow for blow. She was at a disadvantage by sheer size alone. Neither party wanted to injure the other. Himeko was simply defending, not attacking. It allowed Daray to slowly back her up until her back was against the wall with nowhere else to go.

In a last ditch effort to get away from Daray, Himeko struck out with her tiny fist. Daray grabbed her wrist and used her own momentum to spin her around. He trapped her next to his body in a vise-like grip.

Daray inhaled her scent, and it had his beast rising to the surface once more. His animal side was clawing at him demanding that he claim his mate. He had never let himself be ruled by instinct alone, but in that moment he had to agree that claiming Himeko seemed to be the best course of action.

He still had enough of his rational mind to know that such a claiming would be better served in their quarters instead of a cargo bay. He threw Himeko over his shoulder. She pounded on his back and cursed him in several languages, though she seemed to slip into her native Japanese for most of it. He knew that for her to override the translation device implanted in her brain, she had to really be emotional.

He stalked through the crowds of gawking people as he marched towards their quarters. He smacked Himeko's attractive bottom as her insults became more colorful. He let no one deter him from his goal, not even the loud guffaw of Alaric at the sight of the normally stately pair.

CHAPTER NINETEEN

Daray stalked through the door of their shared quarters.

"Computer, secure entrance authorization Daray Nardo alpha two five."

"Entrance secured," the room answered.

Daray walked through to the sleeping area and tossed Himeko on the bed. God she was so beautiful with her dark, flashing eyes as she brushed her disheveled hair from her face. He imagined that this was the way she looked when she had been thoroughly debauched. He just stared down at her as she set herself to rights again.

"What in the five hells was that Daray?" Himeko demanded.

Daray trapped her chin in his large hand and leaned in so their lips almost touched. "You are mine, Himeko. No other man gets to touch you." His grip tightened as she tried to pull away from him.

Himeko used a pressure point in Daray's elbow to break his hold. "You don't get to decide that, Daray."

Daray growled as he pinned her to the bed. He inhaled the sweet fragrance of Himeko's arousal. "Your body knows to whom you belong."

Himeko hooked her leg around Daray and flipped them until she was straddling his hips. She looked down at him and Daray could see a flash of vulnerability that she was normally able to hide behind her serene mask.

"I don't understand you, Daray. Hot and cold…. Sometimes you act like you want me; then other times you can't seem to get away from me fast enough."

Daray frowned as her eyes shimmered with unshed tears. He was confused. He always wanted her, so much so that he had verged on dishonoring her by human standards. Himeko slid off of his body and sat on the bed facing away from him. She wrapped her arms around herself as she tried to contain the tears in her eyes.

Daray's anger swiftly changed to concern. He could feel the hurt rolling off of Himeko in waves, but he didn't understand it. He reached for her, but she flinched away. Somehow, he was the source of her pain and he had to find a way to make it right.

"Enough."

One word. Daray heard his entire world shatter in that word. He could feel Himeko walking away from him in that word. Unacceptable. He wouldn't allow it to end this way.

He punched the mattress. "We belong together, Himeko. I know you feel it too."

She suddenly stood and turned on him with clenched fists. "What kind of game are you playing, Daray? Bring me close then push me away. I'm tired of it!" Himeko's voice continued to rise with each word.

Daray reached for her only to have her bat his

hand away. His mate was rejecting him. He had enough honor left that he knew he should walk away at this point, but he could still smell her arousal behind the pain in her voice. He knew that this was somehow his fault though he didn't understand how, but the human way was obviously not working. So it was time to do this the Vukasin way.

Daray grabbed her hand. While he held her wrist gently, his grip was unbreakable. He tugged her down until he could trap her beneath his body. He remembered her tricks and used his bulk to pin her legs. He used his other hand to pull her other wrist over her head and used one large hand to pin her arms there.

Himeko twisted and fought beneath him and his body responded. Himeko gasped as she felt the long, hard length of him against her thigh. She couldn't help the heat of desire that rushed between her legs.

Daray inhaled deeply and Himeko felt more than heard the deep rumbling growl that escaped. He locked eyes with her and they watched each other's pupils dilate with desire. All of the pain and uncertainty vanished in the heat of their gaze. There was no mistaking the intensity of that look between them.

Himeko couldn't breathe. She had dreamt of a moment very similar to this for well over a year now. She had never let on how she felt about Daray because he had always kept a respectful distance. But that changed when they came to the underwater city.

When he claimed her as mate, even if it had just been a ruse to keep them together, hope had bloomed in her chest. Then that hope died a little each time he rejected her. She was angry, hurt, and confused.

Himeko went slack in his hold. She turned her head to the side to hide the tears that spilled from her eyes. "I can't do this," she whispered.

"Do what, *jinaria*?"

The fire of anger flashed in Himeko's heart. How could this man not know what he was doing to her? Daray has eased his grip when she had started crying. Himeko used his inattention to hook her leg around his and throw her slight weight against him. He hadn't been expecting the move so she was able to flip him beneath her.

Himeko glared at him and growled. Daray's

eyes went wide at the sound. Of course he had seen Himeko get angry, but it had only been in the political realm. Today was the first time that her anger had been directed at him, and so far he managed to bring it out in her twice.

Her hot tears streamed down her face, hitting Daray on his chest. He reached for her.

"*Jinaria?*"

Himeko slapped his hands away. "*Uzai! Kono yarou!*"

Daray knew her emotions must be running high since she overrode the translator to yell at him in her native language. He wasn't sure what she had said to him, but he was fairly certain that is wasn't anything flattering.

"You give me hope only to reject me," Himeko sobbed as her tiny fist beat at Daray's chest. It didn't hurt; she was just beating out her frustrations and anger. Daray knew she could hurt him if she really wanted to.

"I've never rejected you, Himeko," Daray replied quietly.

Both fists slammed down on his chest,

causing Daray to wince. Okay, that hurt.

"Never rejected me?" Himeko's voice growled. "When I tried to kiss you, you shoved me away. You told me that you loved me only to run out of the room like your pants were on fire. You pull me close then push me away. Every time you do something that makes me think you have feelings of more than friendship for me, I wait for the inevitable shove." Himeko clasped her hands in front of her heart. "It hurts, Daray...." Her voice fell back to a whisper and her tears started fresh.

Daray didn't understand what had happened. He had tried to honor her and her planet's customs but somehow ended up hurting her instead. He reached up and pulled her down against his chest. "Enough. Forget the human marriage ceremony."

When Himeko raised her head to ask him what he meant by that, Daray devoured her with his lips. He trapped her within his arms. Himeko didn't even care that he held her so tight that she had trouble breathing because it felt like he never wanted to let her go.

"I am Vukasin," he declared between kisses.

"You are," Himeko agreed.

"I will claim you as a Vukasin should."

"Thank the gods!"

Himeko wrapped her arms around his neck and pulled him back down into a deep kiss. Himeko tore at Daray's shirt, desperate to feel his skin against hers. Now that they were on the same page, she needed him desperately.

Daray growled and whipped his shirt over his head. Himeko reached up and traced the planes of muscle across his chest, leaving a trail of fire burning in her wake. He ripped Himeko's clothes from her, shredding them at the seams. He was desperate to see her. He had held himself in check for so long that he felt like he had gone mad now that he was allowed to touch her.

Himeko toed off her boots while she was still under Daray. She lifted her hips as he tore her clothes from her to help him fully reveal herself to him. Once she was laid bare, Daray stopped and just gazed at her as if she were a precious work of art. In that moment, she felt both powerful and truly beautiful.

"Beautiful, *jinaria mio*," Daray whispered in reverence.

Himeko threw him a sensual smile and cupped his hardness through his pants. "You have too many clothes on." She reached up and nipped at his chin.

Daray flipped Himeko over and traced the pulse of her neck with his teeth and tongue. "I'm not sure I can be gentle like you deserve, Princess. The beast wants his mate."

Himeko arched, up pressing her backside against his clothed manhood. "Who said I wanted gentle?"

Daray roared and stood up. He quickly divested himself of the last barrier between him and his woman. Himeko had raised herself onto all fours. He silky hair cascaded down one shoulder to puddle in the bed as she gave him a sultry look over the other shoulder. Her eyes widened slightly at the sight of his impressive erection before her face melted into a self-satisfied smile. She held out her hand and beckoned to him, and like a pet on a leash Daray came to her. It was humbling to know that the delicate creature before him held so much sway.

It was even more humbling to see Himeko bare her neck for him. The beast in his nature roared with triumph as she put herself in that submissive pose. She was offering him everything he had ever dreamed of, and she did it willingly.

He drunk in the sight of his woman. Daray's instincts were riding him hard, but he wanted to memorize this moment because it was the moment his life changed forever. His fingers traced the intricate design inked across Himeko's back. He had seen the tattoo only one other time, by accident, and it fascinated him. Daray's research told him that the image of the burning bird was a phoenix. Earth legends say that the bird died in flames only to be reborn in beauty again. It was the perfect symbol for Himeko, who rose from slavery to be a diplomat for an entire civilization.

Daray smiled as Himeko shivered at his touch. He ran his fingers through the long length of her silky black hair. He vowed that one day he would spend all of his time touching and learning the feel of Himeko's body, but tonight was not the night for such gentle knowledge. He fisted his hand in her hair and forced her to turn her head.

His kiss was brutal. Himeko could feel his canine teeth expanding as the beast that lurked within pushed to the surface. She loved that he was affected by her to the point that his other half was pushing to rise. Himeko bit and sucked on Daray's bottom lip as he pulled away from her.

Himeko could see him struggling for control. She didn't want his control. He gave his control to everyone else. She wanted him to lose control because she knew that would only happen with her. She rolled over onto her back, raising up on her arms. The move thrust her small breasts forward. She would never have the curvy frame of some of the other women, but she knew enough of her own appeal to know that the delicate frame with pale skin and midnight hair could mesmerize just as easily.

Daray watched her intently. He knew that every move was meant to entrance him, and it did. But he didn't care. She did this for him. She became this sensual creature only for him. Part of him wanted to watch her like this forever. The other part wanted to bury his shaft up to the hilt.

He reached out to run a hand up her delicate leg. His other reached out to cup her cheek. The feral part of him rumbled with contentment as she leaned into his touch. The hand on her leg found the apex of her thighs. He had smelled her arousal as she turned over, but now he could feel the evidence of it on his fingers.

"You deserve a beautiful slow seduction,

jinaria. I doubt I can accomplish slow," Daray said as he inhaled that wonderful scent that was uniquely Himeko. A shadow of doubt crossed his mind that because of her delicate size he would hurt her.

Himeko saw the shadow pass through his gaze and knew that Daray was overthinking again. She swore to herself that she was going to figure out a way to short-circuit that part of his brain until he was lost in the moment. She placed a tiny hand on top of his and pushed his fingers deeper into her core. She smiled at his sharp intake of breath.

"Fast and rough can be beautiful too, my love."

My love…two simple words, but they shattered Daray's reality. Himeko loved him. The shock of it froze him in place. He didn't come back to the present until he felt Himeko's tongue lick up his shaft. He hadn't even realized that she had moved. When her mouth engulfed him in her warm heat he nearly phased in response. He hadn't lost control of his beastly nature like that since he was an adolescent.

Watching Himeko was a thing of beauty, but his beast wanted its mate. Daray pulled Himeko from him, and she nipped the tip of his shaft with her teeth as punishment. He chuckled. Earth's famous Shakespeare was quoted as saying "Though she be but little, she is fierce." He could have been writing about Himeko.

Daray laid her back down, his large hands tracing her slight curves until he brought her hands back over her head. With one large palm, he gripped both of them to hold her there. She had teased him to the point of shattering his control. It was his turn.

Daray's lips and teeth played across her skin until every nerve ending was on fire with sensation. Himeko tried to tug her hands free to touch him; she needed to feel more, but his grip was immovable. She needed….

"Please, Daray," Himeko breathlessly cried.

Daray nuzzled her neck, and with one swift thrust sheathed himself into her wet heat. He let out a groan. He was home; this sensation here would always be home to him and he knew that Himeko was the only woman who could give it to him. Daray had been no saint; he had gone to the pleasure houses like most men of his species did, but those acts paled in comparison to what he felt here and now with Himeko.

Himeko cried out at his invasion, but she quickly melted into Daray. He filled every part of her just like she knew he would. He stretched her almost to the point of pain, but that slight bite just added to the sensations swirling through her body. She was so close with just a single thrust, but she needed more. Himeko rolled her hips, moving her body along his steel-like length. Daray took the hint and began moving.

His pace started out slow, a wonderful torture. Himeko closed her eyes and moaned his name. He felt so good, so right, but she still needed more. She flexed her fingers. She really wished that Daray would release her hands, even though a part of her loved that he had taken control. Himeko smiled and licked her lips as she stared up at Daray. His face contorted as the phase pushed forward. It told Himeko that he may think he is the one in control, but she had power of her own over him.

She leaned up and nuzzled his neck. She inhaled his scent and heard him growl as she licked at his pulse point. Then she bit him hard at that point. It was a primal move she was claiming him as her mate. She may not have the same enzymes that he did, but the move called his beast to the surface.

She bit him! The beast roared at her daring.

She was challenging his dominance and she knew it. The rational part of Daray was lost behind instincts as old as time. He let go of her wrists and flipped Himeko over and started pounding into her. He knew by her chuckle that that was exactly what she wanted. He reached around to tweak her nipple. Her chuckle turned into a moan as he soothed away the sting with a caress of his large hands.

Himeko arched her back, pushing back against Daray's thrusts. His hands moved from her breasts down her taunt stomach and through the darks curls. It was such an erotic feeling to have the heat of his hand cover her mound as his shaft pistoned in and out of her. She moved her slender hips against his touch, silently begging him to touch that place she knew would make her explode.

Daray kept up a brutal pace. He could feel Himeko's hot sheath tightening around him, and he knew that she was close to climax. His jaw contorted as the beastly side of him got ready. He watched her for the perfect moment. She tossed her dark hair over one shoulder and the creamy length of her beautiful neck was exposed to him. She closed her eyes and leaned her head to one side, offering herself to him. Daray flicked that little bud and her core nearly strangled his manhood as she shouted her climax.

In that moment, the beast struck, sinking his teeth into that spot where neck met shoulder. His teeth broke the skin as the enzymes that would tie them together until one of them perished flowed into his mate. His mate…Himeko was truly his now. This wasn't one of his fantasies. He tongued his bite to speed the healing as Himeko collapsed beneath him.

Daray's face returned to that of the man. "Himeko?"

"Give me a minute." Himeko's voice was muffled against the cover of the bed.

Daray laid down next to Himeko, drawing her into his arms.

She curled into him and sighed. "That was wonderful."

Daray cupped her cheek. He raised her eyes to his. She had such beautiful eyes. They were so dark that he felt like he could fall into them forever. He leaned down and kissed each eyelid, her cheek, the edge of her lips…until he captured her lips entirely. He deepened the kiss, trying to meld their souls together. "That was just the beginning."

"By the moons, I hope so."

Daray spent the rest of the night convincing her.

CHAPTER TWENTY

Himeko woke surrounded by warmth. She tried to get up from the bed only to have Daray's arm tighten around her. She rolled over to examine the man who was now her mate. She rubbed at the bite at the juncture of her neck and shoulder. She had always suspected that there was a passionate man beneath the calm exterior, but even she had been surprised at his intensity.

Himeko reached up and traced the stubble on Daray's chin. She liked that she was the only one to see the disheveled look. It was like a piece of himself that he gave only to her, just like her tattoo was a piece of herself that she showed only to him. She smiled at the memory of him tracing her tattoo with gentle kisses after their rough and frantic session of sex.

They had talked long into the night, and Himeko chuckled at the fact that their whole misunderstanding was because Daray was trying to court her the human way. Of course he made the mistake of just reading about religious custom instead of actually talking to a human about what the 'human way' was really about.

Daray's eyes remained closed, but a small smile graced his lips and his arms tightened around Himeko.

"I can feel you thinking, *jinaria*."

Himeko nipped at his chin and was about to tell him what she had been thinking about when an alarm blared through their quarters, startling them. Daray rolled off the bed to his feet and Himeko followed suit.

"What's going on?" Himeko asked as she quickly dressed. She sighed at the thought of not getting a shower, but it couldn't be helped.

"I don't know. Alaric said the alarms were only to inform of an attack."

Himeko stood up, her shirt half hanging off

of her frame. "Do you think the ruling family has found me?"

Daray shoved his last foot into his boot. "I don't know, but we better find out. Be prepared to call Vukas no matter what is going on. That includes the information on Brandy and her son."

Himeko frowned. She wouldn't let even Daray dictate to her. She needed to make a decision about Brandy, but in the end she would do what she thought was right. She just wasn't sure what that was right now.

Daray and Himeko rushed from their quarters. The citizens of the underwater city were rushing to their assigned stations during a disaster. Daray and Himeko didn't have assignments, so they headed out to look for Alaric to see how they could help.

They found him in the retrieval pod area. Water was rushing in from a dangerous-looking crack in the city's protective shell. Engineers were frantically trying to stem the flow of water and repair the shell. Himeko was worried it was a losing battle as the crack continued to travel upwards as they closed up the bottom.

"What in the five hells happened?" Daray demanded from Alaric as he watched the disaster unfold.

"Evidently the ruling family is tired of the 'sea monster' snatching slaves." Alaric heaved a heavy sigh. "So with no regard to how their actions impact the environment, they have started scanning the depths using sound wave."

"Sonar? I didn't think sonar could reach these depths," Himeko said.

"The normal scanning device couldn't, but they seem to have found a way to greatly increase its power. However, it is driving the dalli fish and leviathans crazy. They have started attacking the shell of our city." Alaric shouted an order to the crew racing to save their lives.

"It is probably painful to them. On my planet, numerous studies showed that the use of sonar had a detrimental effect on the whales, huge animals that swam our oceans. Some even believed that it was killing them off."

Alaric turned to Himeko. "I'm asking you again to intercede on our behalf with your government. One way or another we are going to be discovered soon. Whether it is because they find the cities with their scanning or because we have to evacuate to the surface. If we are found, the people in the cities will either be killed or enslaved once again. I know you don't trust me, but at least help my people."

Himeko sighed. Alaric was right. Even if she didn't ask for Ghaleb's involvement in this conflict, she would have to call him to retrieve herself and the others. She knew Ghaleb well enough to know that he would want to collect any of the Vukasins that had been enslaved by the Polaxians.

"I make no promises, Alaric, but I will contact my government."

"Down that hall." Alaric pointed ahead of them. "Take a left at the cross hall and go to the end. It is one of the private communications rooms. You can call me on the city intercom if you need me."

Himeko turned and quickly moved down the hall, with Daray following. It didn't take them long to get to the room Alaric directed them to.

"Do you know how to encrypt a transmission, Daray?" Himeko asked. She was adapting to the technology of her new reality pretty well, but she still had difficulty with some of the more technical things.

Daray moved to the console and set up the transmission. It didn't take long for Reijo's face to appear on the view screen.

"Am I a fugitive at the moment?" Daray asked.

Reijo chuckled. "By bringing home almost the entire crew of the diplomatic mission, Ghaleb had to consider you a hero, especially since you did it without starting a war."

"Yeah, about that not starting a war…."

"I knew your appearance was too good to be true. Give me a minute and I will get Ghaleb and Kavi."

Reijo left the screen and Daray turned to Himeko. "About Brandy and her son…."

Himeko shook her head, "They are safer if no one knows they exist."

"But—"

"No, Daray. I'm not going to betray her

trust."

Reijo reentered the screen with Ghaleb and Kavi.

"I'm so glad to see you alive, Himeko. Megan was really worried about you." Ghaleb smiled.

"I would have let you know I was alright sooner if I could have, Ghaleb. We have a bit of a situation, and it could have far-reaching consequences." Himeko took a deep breath to detail what they had fallen into.

When she was about to speak again, Daray blurted out, "We have found your son, Ghaleb."

Everyone went silent, staring at Daray, but only Himeko's eyes held an angry gaze. Everyone else looked more shocked.

"I don't have a son, Daray."

With the cat out of the bag, Himeko gave in to the inevitable. "Daray is correct. We have found the first human female that stumbled onto Vukas. She was enslaved by the Tanis, along with several others. The Tanis have had a thriving slave trade for years."

"What does this have to do with me having a son I knew nothing about?"

"You will have to get the particulars from the woman in question. Unlike Daray, I will not break a confidence. But regardless, her son is also yours. DNA tests confirmed it."

Ghaleb sank into his chair, eyes wide with shock. "A son…I have a son."

"Your son is a secondary issue to the one we currently have at hand." Himeko brought Ghaleb back to the conversation at hand.

"What could be more important than finding out I have a son?"

"We have a situation here that could cost the lives of thousands, including your son. But your involvement might start a war. However, without your help there is a good chance that we will either perish or be enslaved once more."

Ghaleb's eyes suddenly went hard. "I don't care what I have to do. My son and his mother are coming home."

CHAPTER TWENTY-ONE

The alarms started blaring once again. This time they were accompanied by a computerized voice.

"Evacuation procedure alpha. Quickly proceed to your assigned escape pod. Evacuation procedure alpha...."

"What's going on?" Ghaleb demanded.

"Evidently the engineers couldn't fix the damage. We are being told to evacuate." Himeko stood and bowed to Ghaleb. "We will contact you again as soon as we can."

Himeko turned off the transmission in the middle of Ghaleb's questions and left the communications room. Daray hurried her along with a hand in the small of her back guiding her through the gathered crowd. He could have easily made it to the pod in half the time as Himeko, but he refused to move from her side in the frantic crush.

A few scuffles broke out among the frightened populace at the pods, but most shuffled through silently with wide, frightened eyes. Even with water steadily rising at their feet, they moved in quiet worry. That told Himeko more than anything else just what kind of horrors these poor people had already experienced.

Himeko spotted Raylan on the far side of the pod storage platform waving them over frantically. Both Himeko and Daray moved as quickly as they could through the crush. Raylan ushered them into the escape pod.

Himeko had been expecting tight confines similar to the pod that dragged her down to the underwater city. She was pleasantly surprised to find that the escape pod was more of a submarine, with a control center and serval seats around the interior.

Alaric was already inside their pod at the controls.

Himeko looked at several unfamiliar faces and frowned. "Where are Brandy and her son?"

Alaric answered without turning from his task at the controls, "They were assigned to a pod group closer to their quarters. Don't worry; she knows what to do."

With no other choice, Himeko and Daray took seats and secured themselves. They heard a loud cracking noise and the pod shook violently.

"Looks like the temporary repairs are in catastrophic failure." Alaric hit a control on the console. "Report!"

Several voices were heard across the communications; many said they were loaded and ready, a few still had people loading.

"Hurry it up, shove as many in as you can if you have to. We have to leave now!"

Alaric turned his attention to entering the launch information. A thunderous explosion was heard and a few voices on the communicator screamed before falling eerily silent. Himeko watched Alaric, and she saw him close his eyes and blink back tears for those they obviously just lost. Roaring waters could be heard outside of their pod doors and their pod shuddered with the force of several metric tons of water rushing over them.

"Launch!" Alaric called into the communicator.

He hit the controls and their pod disengaged from the moorings. He used the controls to guide the sub away from the underwater city. Himeko could see several other pods zipping by out of the window at the front of their vessel. She had assumed that they would be heading to the surface and was surprised to see various vessels heading into deeper waters, while others headed in the opposite direction. None of the escape vessels seemed to be going to the surface.

Alaric guided their ship and turned it around to see the destruction of what had been his home for a few decades. Himeko was startled when the body of a man hit their window, lifeless eyes wide with terror. Alaric blinked back tears at the loss of life, but he watched as his city was completely destroyed. The dome had collapsed around the area that the dalli fish and leviathans had cracked. The lights of the city glowed for a while and then blinked a few times before falling into permanent darkness.

Alaric turned the sub away from the remains

of his home. He punched the accelerator, throwing the occupants deeper into their seats.

"Are we not heading to the surface?" Daray asked.

"It's still too dangerous for us to be on the surface," Alaric answered. "Our emergency procedures have us splitting up among the other underwater cities for the time being."

Alaric turned the vessel on a hard right to avoid hitting the monstrous leviathan in their path. Evidently navigating the deeper waters was going to take some skill and concentration.

Himeko looked at Daray and he shook his head. They had several questions that needed to be answered, but they would have to wait until they arrived at their destination.

CHAPTER TWENTY-TWO

The refugees arrived at another underwater city. This city was much smaller than the one they had come from. As a result, many people were forced to sleep in the common areas, and resources were closely guarded and rationed.

Himeko and Daray walked in on Alaric and the leaders of this city as they discussed their future.

"…another three weeks if we are lucky. After that there will be nothing left."

Alaric spotted the Vukasin pair and dismissed his fellow leader.

"Have you located Brandy and Alex?" Daray

asked.

"I'm afraid that as best we can tell they were captured by those on the surface." Alaric moved to a side board and poured himself a glass of fiery liquor.

"I thought the pods were supposed to go to the other rebel cities." Himeko took a seat and motioned for the men to do the same. The restless pacing was getting on her nerves.

Alaric sat across from her. "They were, but it appears that the surface has finally gotten suspicious. Their sonar scans had been concentrated on the destroyed city for quite a while. It was one of the reasons that the wildlife in the area became so aggressive." He sighed. "It doesn't look like they were able to definitively figure out what they were seeing, but they knew it was something."

Alaric stopped and took a swallow of his drink.

"They are still scanning, aren't they?" Himeko asked.

Alaric nodded. "They have turned to a systematic search of the oceans. Some of the pods were spotted and captured because of that…including Brandy's pod."

Daray swore and Himeko sighed.

"We need to find her and Alex, but we have a more pressing problem, don't we?" Himeko leveled a frown at Alaric. "When were you going to tell us that the supplies were running out?"

Alaric wiped a hand down his face. "Honestly it isn't going to matter much because our estimates show that the surface is going to find this base before we run out of supplies. We have days at most before the sonar searches reach this area. If you can't get your government to help us, then all is lost."

"We need to check in with our government anyway." Himeko stood. "I can't make any promises, but I will see what I can do. Where will you be if I need to find you?"

Alaric stood up and returned his glass to the side board. "I'll be in the main storage area cataloging weapons and supplies." He turned back to Himeko and Daray. "You can use the communication equipment in the control center. It's the only place on this base that has off-world communication ability. Just tell them I sent you."

Himeko nodded and she and Daray left the

room to head towards the control center.

"You know Ghaleb is going to tear this planet apart looking for his son," Daray said.

"That's what I am afraid of," Himeko sighed. "It looks like we are going to war one way or another, but without a plan and intelligence on the enemy we could be walking into a war we may lose."

Daray remained quiet until they reached the command center. Guards stopped them as they tried to enter the room.

"We need to speak with your officer on duty," Daray said.

A woman who seemed to be a cross between a Polaxian and a Ludian stepped forward.

"That would be me. I'm Commander Tia."

"Alaric sent us here to send an off-world communication. It is a diplomatic transmission. Is there any way we could make this transmission in private?" Himeko asked.

"I'm afraid that would require clearing the entire command center, and even if Alaric vouches for you I am not comfortable leaving my command in the hands of strangers."

"I understand. Would it be an acceptable compromise if we allowed you to remain during the transmission? Though you have to understand that you cannot speak of anything you hear." Himeko wasn't really sure she could trust this new individual to keep secrets, but in a matter of days it wouldn't matter one way or the other if the surface captured them all.

The commander tapped her chin thoughtfully and then turned to call Alaric on the communication array. While he wasn't this city's leader, he seemed to be the one that all of the separate rebel areas turned to for leadership. Whatever Tia and Alaric discussed seemed to satisfy her because she cleared the room temporarily.

"I can set up the communication transmission if you give me the frequency you need."

Tia raised an eyebrow when Daray requested an encrypted transmission, but she did as he asked. Soon Reijo was on the screen before them.

"Thank the gods you are safe." Reijo sighed. "We feared the worst after your last transmission."

"Where is Ghaleb. We need to speak to him urgently," Himeko cut in.

Reijo groaned, "He has already left the planet and is heading towards the Polaxian home world to retrieve his son."

"Does he not realize that he is going to start a war before we are ready by doing that?" Himeko growled.

Reijo gave a bit of a chuckle. "Well, Kavi is with him, and I believe they are going to meet up with your friend Se'lak, Daray."

"Good, then we might avoid unnecessary bloodshed," Daray said. "However, there is a problem. Brandy and Alex are missing, presumed captured by the surface faction."

Reijo swore vividly. "Ghaleb is going to tear that world apart looking for them."

"If they are still on Polax. The Tanis have a strong presence on this planet as well. They have been searching for the pair since they escaped," Himeko added.

"Oh this just keeps getting better." Reijo ran a hand through his hair and pulled it in agitation.

"Anything else you want to drop on me?"

"We have just a couple of days before the surface discovers this base as well. We are preparing for battle, but honestly the people here are out gunned and out manned. If Vukas is going to ally with the rebel faction, they need to get moving fast." Himeko delivered the news without inflection.

"Ghaleb and Megan had already made an executive decision to aid the rebels. We are hoping to crush the slave trade once and for all in this galaxy. Not to mention, it makes sense to weaken the Tanis ties to their allies."

"That good to hear," Daray sighed with relief.

"Reijo, you and I both know that mobilizing a force of the size we would need is going to take time," Himeko added.

Reijo nodded, "I doubt we will be able to get to you in a couple of days. I would estimate closer to a week before we could come to your aid. Are you going to be able to hold out?"

"We will have to." Himeko sighed. "Get word to Ghaleb about Brandy and her son. We don't need him getting caught in the crossfire."

"Se'lak is good at what he does. Information is his area of expertise. If anyone can find out where they are, he can. Just convince Ghaleb to listen to the man," Daray added.

"All right. Stay safe and I will get the troops mobilized as fast as I can."

"Thank you, Reijo," Himeko said.

The communication array clicked off and Tia turned to Himeko.

"Is it true? Are we going to war?"

Himeko sighed. "You should really talk to your higher ups to get the specifics, but it is true that the underwater cities are no longer secure."

Tia nodded and turned back to the console. She started pulling up information regarding the city's weapons supply and evacuation. Himeko could appreciate a woman focused on practical planning to deal with the fear of the future.

Himeko and Daray turned to leave the command center when Tia called out once more.

"Will the Vukasins really come to our aid?"

Daray turned and answered, "Reijo doesn't lie."

Tia nodded.

CHAPTER TWENTY-THREE

Himeko was quickly marching down the hall. Daray could see the tension radiating from her and he wasn't sure what had made her angry. She had been like this since they had left the command center. She seemed to know where she was going, however. Daray realized that memorizing the layout of new spaces was an advantage to a diplomat. Himeko was on a mission and all he could do was follow along.

Daray found himself entering the armory behind Himeko. The guards at the door tried to stop their entrance, but a single quelling look from Himeko had them backing off. Daray grinned as he followed behind his mate. He loved the fact that such a tiny woman could give off such an intimidating aura.

"Alaric!" Himeko barked as she marched through the shelves of weaponry.

They found the rebel leader in the far back corner cataloguing ammunition with a few of his men. Daray frowned. It appeared that much of their ordnances were old-fashioned projectile weaponry. That kind of fire power would be a liability in an underwater city, as a stray bullet could damage the shell that protected them.

Alaric raised his head at Himeko's shout and waved off his subordinates. Himeko marched right up to him until she had to look up at the man. Despite her petite stature, Alaric still took a step back when she advanced on him.

Himeko had her finger in Alaric's chest, poking him for emphasis as she dressed him down. Daray rubbed his chest in sympathy. The Polaxian was probably going to have a bruise there before Himeko finished her lecture.

She was outraged that Alaric hadn't briefed his officers about the impending fight. She was adamant that the people needed as much time to prepare as possible. She dismissed Alaric's argument that they were mostly women and children.

By this time, Alaric had started to get angry. It was obvious he wasn't used to having someone question his decisions. His men heard their leader shouting and came running. Daray moved to protect Himeko from the guards. He grabbed one of the guards and tossed him to the ground, but another rushed past him.

"Himeko!" Daray lifted his head to warn her, but he needn't have worried. Himeko used the guard's own momentum against him and flipped him over her shoulder. She grabbed the man's arm and twisted, placing her foot in his back for leverage. The man was easily twice her size, but she had him on the ground crying out in pain.

"You don't think woman can fight? Have you ever seen a mother defend its young?" Himeko tossed the arm of the poor guard away. She shoved him back to the ground with her boot as he tried to rise. "You are leaving them for slaughter if you don't prepare them for what is to come."

"We have two days at the most. What do you think we can accomplish in that time to prepare them?" Alaric growled. "Why do you think I wanted the Vukasin's help?"

"You mean you wanted Vukas to fight your battle for you," Daray cut in.

Alaric didn't look Daray in the eye.

Himeko sighed and finally let the guard on the floor up. "Alaric, if you truly want to change your world, you cannot rely on others to do the dirty work for you. You and your people need to be at the epicenter or this change, otherwise it will never last."

"What did your government say?"

Himeko shook her head, and Daray kept quiet. She looked Alaric in the eye with a glare. "Gather your commanders and civic leaders. We will discuss what is about to occur with everyone or not at all."

"Himeko…." Alaric growled. Daray could see he didn't like seeing Himeko taking over, but the man needed a reality check. Keeping a hidden people going was going to be a lot different than leading a people in war. Daray knew that if he didn't change and adapt then Alaric would need to be replaced if his people weren't going to be wiped out. It was callous, but Alaric needed to understand that Vukas's involvement wasn't for his benefit but to save those it considered its citizens. If Alaric's cause turned out to be a lost cause, the Vukasin government would leave them to their fate out of necessity. But if the Polaxian leader could prove he had what it took to lead a planet towards change then he could find a strong ally in Vukas.

"Alaric, I am not some green girl that you can intimidate. We either do it this way or the only Vukasins you will see are those here to pick up their citizens and get the hell out of Dodge."

"What does that even mean?" Alaric asked.

"Old Earth saying meaning leave as quickly as possible from a dangerous situation," Daray clarified.

Alaric's stood there huffing as he tried to stare down Himeko and Daray. The pair just crossed their arms and waited. It was kind of funny how their mannerisms mirrored each other. *We are a unified pair*, Daray thought.

Of course we are. We are mates after all.

Himeko's voice whispered through Daray's mind and it took every ounce of willpower not to show his shock in his outward appearance. He had heard that the human women took to the mating bond faster than a Vukasin woman did, but he hadn't expected such a strong connection so soon.

Alaric's eyes swung back and forth between the pair. Finally his shoulders slumped and he pinched the bridge of his nose, trying to relieve the headache building there. Himeko recognized the signs of the strain Alaric was under. She also knew that it was going to get much worse before it got better.

He is the last of his family. He's trying to live up to his legacy.

Himeko suppressed a smile as Daray chose to address her in their intimate way.

You should know better than anyone that one man can't govern. He has to learn to ask for help and to delegate tasks to those who can accomplish them.

I agree with you, Himeko, but what do you want me to do about it?

Himeko fell silent even in her mind. Polaxians were proud men. Alaric may respect her and her position as a diplomat, but she knew from experience that men from patriarchal societies resented even good advice if it came from the feminine quarter. Given enough time, Himeko knew that she had a talent for "becoming one of the boys." But time was something they were running out of.

Polaxians like Alaric reminded her a lot of the Nardo clan when she first met them. Like the Nardo clan….

"That's it!" Himeko startled both of the men.

"Excuse me?" Alaric eyed Himeko with uncertainty.

Daray, he isn't going to listen to me without resentment. His entire culture conditioned him to that. I don't have time to recondition him so he would take me seriously. But you he will take seriously if for no other reason you are a powerful male who is responsible for his people just like Alaric. He can relate to you.

Himeko….

Himeko shoved Daray towards Alaric.

"Alaric, Daray needs to talk to you leader to leader."

Himeko raised an eyebrow at Daray and gestured towards the Polaxian royal.

Daray cleared his throat, "That's right. I would like to discuss your plans in regards to the upcoming battle. I trained with our planet's top general. I might be able to offer some advice on battle strategy."

Himeko sent Daray the impression of a huge smile and a warm hug. *Smooth. You might have a talent as a diplomat after all.*

I do have to keep up with my mate after all.

Himeko turned to head back to their quarters with a wave when she stopped suddenly.

"Um…where are we sleeping?" She turned towards the men.

Alaric chuckled, "We gave you and your mate the last private quarters. Section Alpha room 765. I'm afraid it is only a single room for sleeping though."

"That's fine." She turned to Daray and gave him a kiss before waving goodbye to the men.

CHAPTER TWENTY-FOUR

Almost immediately after Himeko and Daray had briefed the various leaders of the rebel faction, they found themselves handing out weapons to the general populace of the underwater city. The people had been instructed to gather only what they could carry in a single pack and then report to receive arms.

The destruction of Alaric's main base had showed everyone that trying to remain hidden could end up as a death sentence. Instead, scouts had been sent to the surface to find a suitable location to make their stand.

Daray had insisted that Raylan be among the scouts. He was still a little awkward around his childhood friend because he still had suspicions that Raylan was attracted to Himeko. Himeko wished Raylan would come clean to Daray about his sexual preferences, but it wasn't her secret to tell.

She handed the last gun to a young woman who appeared to be from Ludus Prime. Even by their standards she was tiny and looked so very young. Himeko closed her eyes against the image of the young woman dead and bloodied. They were going to war; it was a possible future.

"That's the last of them." Daray came over and wrapped his arms around her waist, hugging her from behind. Since they officially became mates he had become much more tactile. Himeko was still adjusting to the changes in their relationship.

I can hear your thoughts you know, Daray chuckled in her mind.

Himeko promptly sent him a picture of her elbowing him in the ribs, only to have Daray laugh out loud.

"How can you be so cheerful when so many are going to die?"

Himeko wasn't unfamiliar with death. Assassinations and punishments were common things in the family she grew up in. But that was a systematic death…one life for the good of many. She had killed in the arena Listar had thrown her into; she killed to survive. These people were walking into slaughter.

Daray turned her around and cupped her cheek, drawing her eyes to his face. She loved his face. It was strong like he was, but his eyes carried a peace that never failed to calm her. She needed that peace at that moment.

"These people are doing the same thing that you did in the arena…. They are fighting for survival." Daray stroked her cheek with his thumb.

"I'm scared, Daray," Himeko admitted. "These people aren't soldiers; they haven't even been properly trained. Can we really hold out until Reijo gets here?"

"We are mates, Himeko, so I cannot lie to you. Even if I did, you would know." Daray hugged Himeko closer. "The odds are against us, but I have seen battles turn simply because one side believed in their cause more than the other. Alaric's people are fighting for their freedom and the freedom of their children. Our enemy is fighting to keep profits flowing. Which side do you think will fight harder?"

Daray looked deeply into Himeko's eyes; she could feel him moving through her mind. When he spoke again, she felt his conviction not just in his words but through her body and soul where he had filled her mind.

"I promise as long as there is breath in me, I will battle to keep you safe."

Himeko stood on her tiptoes and kissed Daray. She poured all of herself into that kiss.

"I promise as long as there is breath in me, I will battle to keep *you* safe."

It was a strange wedding ceremony, but the exchange of those vows felt more meaningful than any ceremony with a fancy dress and cake, to Himeko. They had promised to be there for each other until death took them away. It was the essence of what the human marriage ceremony was meant to be.

Himeko loved Daray and had wanted to be his mate. She knew in his eyes that the mating bite and their psychic connection were proof enough that they were irrevocably bound together for life. She had accepted that, but somewhere in the recesses of her mind she hadn't quite felt like his wife. It wasn't until this moment that she realized that the exchange of vows had meant so much to her.

"When this is over, we will have a ceremony in front of our friends and clan." Daray kissed the top of her head.

"Reading my mind again?"

"You have to admit that it is a good skill to have since you have a habit of keeping so much to yourself." Daray chuckled before becoming serious again. "You don't have to face everything alone, Himeko. I'm here; lean on me sometimes."

Himeko wrapped her arms around Daray's waist and pulled him tight to her. "I love you, you know."

Daray wrapped his arms around Himeko and squeezed. "I love you too."

"You know I can read your mind too…. You have some pretty interesting ideas up in there." Himeko stepped away to throw him a saucy grin.

"Oh? Which ideas are those?" Daray grinned back.

"Well, the one with that gun crate over there

is pretty interesting." Himeko walked towards the crate with a sexy sway in her hips.

"I'm fairly certain that idea came from you." Daray chuckled but he stalked behind her towards the crate.

"Hmm, are you sure? I'm fairly certain that one position was all you." Himeko hopped up on the gun crate and laid back on her elbows with her legs spread.

Daray stepped in between her legs and leaned over to nuzzle and nip at her bared throat. She knew exactly what that pose did to him.

"I was just embellishing on what was already there," he said between teasing kisses.

"Maybe we should see if reality is as good as your imagination," Himeko challenged.

"I'll make reality better than fantasy for you, *jinaria mio*."

Himeko reached up and started to unfasten Daray's shirt as his hands roamed over her body. They were so involved in each other that it took a moment for a noise in the armory to register.

"Ambassador?" a woman's voice called.

Himeko blinked to clear the lust-filled haze and gasped as she realized the state that she and Daray were in. She shoved him away and quickly adjusted her clothing, totally forgetting about the braid in her hair that was now half undone.

Daray kept his amusement to himself as he slowly straightened his own clothing. He would never be embarrassed getting caught loving his mate, though he would try to remember to lock the door next time for his mate's sake.

Tia rounded the stacks of gun crates and jogged up to the pair when she saw them.

"Thank the gods! We have a problem and Alaric asked me to find you. We need to get to the command center right away."

Their lusty interlude temporarily forgotten both Himeko and Daray rushed after Tia. It only took them a matter of minutes to get to the central command center. When they burst in, they could hear the sounds of battle over the comms.

"I told you to just find a location for us to come to the surface." Alaric was screaming at the voice on the other side of the communication.

"I was given orders to find out any information I could about Brandy and her son while we were on the surface."

"I didn't give you that order, Raylan!" Alaric shouted.

Daray and Himeko stepped to the middle of the command center and Daray said, "I gave him that order."

Alaric whipped around with a growl, "Thanks to you, our scouting party has been discovered and they are now prepping for a large-scale search of the seas."

Daray ignored Alaric. "Raylan, did you find a suitable place to make our stand?"

Explosions were heard over the communication line. "We transmitted that information yesterday. I don't believe it was compromised. We were discovered when we tried to get back to the underwater ships."

"Any word on the heir?" Daray continued.

"The information about the *Khala* is hazy at best, but we have reason to believe that the Tanis have already taken the royal family off world."

"*Frex*." Daray heaved a sigh. "You and your men get the hell out of there. Don't try to head back at this point. Evade the enemy and we will meet up once we are on the surface."

"Yes, *Kijani*."

The comm fell silent.

"Why are you giving my men orders without informing me?" Alaric grabbed Daray's shirt and shoved him.

Daray peeled Alaric's fingers from his shirt and glared at the Polaxian. "First off, I gave my men orders. Secondly, you better remember this; my *Khalon* only agreed to involve himself in *your* war because of his son and the mother of his child."

Himeko could hear the whispers of the people around them. Alaric evidently hadn't told anyone why the Vukasins agreed to help. She was seriously considering beating some sense into the man. There was playing things close to the vest and then there was being so tightfisted with information that you lost the trust of the people working for and with you.

But the more pressing matter was that the behavior of those two men was setting up an "us versus them" atmosphere, which was the last thing you wanted among allies because it would often turn them into enemies.

"Why don't they just whip them out and measure?"

Himeko was startled from her thoughts as Tia leaned over and whispered to her. "Excuse me?"

"Men…haven't you noticed how alpha males especially have to challenge each other? It's like they are arguing over who has the biggest set of balls."

Himeko started to giggle. "My planet has a similar saying. I just wasn't expecting to hear it from another species."

Tia smiled at Himeko. "Somehow I don't think people are all the much different when it comes to most things…. Oh, there are cultural references, etiquette, and religion…but under it all people just want to know that they are loved and they matter."

Himeko just stared at Tia until it made the woman uncomfortable.

"What?" Tia frowned.

Himeko smiled. "I was just thinking that you might have a talent for being an amazing diplomat."

Tia blushed and looked away. "They wouldn't let a half breed like me be a diplomat," she mumbled.

Himeko turned Tia towards her and looked into the woman's eyes. "I was brought to Vukas as a slave. I was meant to be nothing more than breeding stock. But one woman stood up against that and I joined her. Then others joined us. Now I am the primary ambassador for Vukas and a voice in the council that helps to decide the direction of our world. You are standing on the cusp of history for Polax. If you rebels are successful in your coup, then a new way of life will have to be created. Ask yourself...do you want someone else creating this new society for you or do you want to be a part of creating it yourself?"

Tia thought for a moment before a grin broke out. "I want to help create it. If we leave it just to the men they will muck it up entirely."

"Alright." Himeko slapped Tia on the back. "Time for your first lesson in diplomacy. Is there somewhere private nearby?"

"There's a conference room across the hall."

"Perfect."

Himeko walked over to the two men who were still making verbal asses of themselves. She reached up and grabbed Daray by the ear and gave it a twist. He very quickly turned to follow her lead to alleviate the pain in his ear.

Alaric started laughing at Daray until Tia grabbed his ear. The entire command center watched as the men were led away by the grim-faced women. A quelling look from Himeko at one man's giggle had the rest of the men silent…at least until they had left.

CHAPTER TWENTY-FIVE

Daray jerked out of Himeko's grip. "What in the five hells...." His voice trailed off at the look of anger that shadowed Himeko's face.

Daray had enough sense to remain silent in the midst of the women's anger. Alaric, however, did not possess that much sense.

"I ought to have you confined to quarters and stripped of your responsibilities, Tia!" the Polaxian practically shouted while rubbing his abused ear. The tantrum continued until Himeko seriously considered gagging the man. He may have been a rebel in hiding, but it was obvious Alaric was too used to getting his way simply because of his royal blood.

To Tia's credit, she didn't flinch or show any emotion while the man raged at her. More and more, Himeko was thinking that Alaric was underutilizing the female. Finally, Himeko had enough.

Alaric didn't even pay attention to the others in the room as he tore into Tia. That could be a fatal mistake even in a room of allies. Alaric was spoiled by the relative safety of the underwater cities, but he was about to enter the treacherous world of the surface and interstellar politics. He needed to learn a few lessons and he needed to learn them fast. Fortunately, Himeko was more than willing to take his entitled attitude down a notch or two.

Himeko saw Tia's eyes shift slightly her way, but she gave no other indication that she saw Himeko move. Himeko swept her leg out to take out Alaric's knee. She was careful to just bring him down and not dislocated it entirely.

Alaric rolled and sprung up with a growl.

"You are a spoiled child, Alaric, who has been playing king in a sheltered kingdom." Himeko advanced on the much larger man. "There is an old Earth saying: 'You are a big fish in a small pond.' You are about to jump head first in the ocean, and unless you change your ways, you are going to be eaten by a leviathan."

"You know nothing of what is going on, female." Alaric sneered that last word.

Himeko shook her head, "That right there is part of what I am talking about."

Tia tried to hold Alaric back, but he was lost in his anger as he charged Himeko.

Daray started to intercept the enraged Polaxian but reluctantly stopped at a shake of Himeko's head. Himeko shifted her stance and grabbed Alaric's arms as he made a grab for her. She used his own momentum to throw him over her shoulder. The last few weeks made her glad that she kept up with her training katas.

Himeko looked down at a stunned Alaric laid out on the ground. "Had enough? Are you willing to listen yet?"

Alaric shoved himself off the ground with a roar.

"Evidently not."

Alaric attacked Himeko, but she used her small size and speed against the Polaxian. It was becoming obvious that Alaric was getting frustrated, as his attacks were becoming more aggressive but at the same time less focused.

Himeko, on the other hand, remained calm and collected. She wasn't a princess but an ice queen. Her expression never changed from one of mild disappointment. She shifted and dodged as if she were performing a choreographed dance. Every once in a while, she would land a blow. Her blows were meant to taunt Alaric, not injure him.

After the fourth or fifth time that Himeko put him on the ground, Alaric finally gave in and just laid there. He stared at the metallic ceiling of the conference room and was glad that the rest of the rebels hadn't seen this one-sided battle with the tiny diplomat.

Himeko leaned over him, her hair cascading over one shoulder. Alaric sighed as he looked up at her but made no move to get off the floor.

"Are you ready to listen, Alaric?" Daray stepped up next to Himeko as he asked the question. "Navigating politics is Himeko's area of expertise."

Daray extended a hand to help the Polaxian to his feet.

"This is war, not politics," Alaric groused.

"War is politics in a concentrated form," Himeko said. "You may have been able to do everything yourself in the underwater cities, but the coming battle is more than convincing Ghaleb and Megan to help you fight. Other than Brandy and her son, Vukas doesn't have an invested interest in what happens on Polax. Though that is changing thanks to the presence of the Tanis."

Alaric stood and walked over to the conference table to sit. He was going to have a fresh set of bruises, but he also knew that Himeko had been pulling her punches. He rubbed a particularly sore spot on his hip. If he learned no other lesson, he learned not to underestimate the delicate looking woman in front of him.

Himeko sat across from Alaric. Daray sat down next to her and reached over to take her hand in his. Only Tia remained standing until Alaric called out to her.

"Since you obviously think that I need to hear what they have to say, you might as well join us, Tia."

Himeko smiled as the woman took her seat

before turning her attention back to Alaric. "You could do worse when it comes to advisors. Tia has proven that she has a level head on her shoulders and is willing to consider several points of view before making a decision. She would make an excellent asset with a little training."

Alaric studied the hybrid woman with new eyes. He knew that she was efficient at organizing the resources of the underwater city, but he had dismissed the idea of her in a governmental role because compared to a pure-bred Polaxian, she was very delicate. He realized that when envisioning his new government, it still was controlled by Polaxians. He had been arrogant in that. Even the Vukasins had integrated the women from Earth into their government, otherwise Himeko wouldn't be here as their diplomat.

Daray watched as several emotions flitted across Alaric's face. The man would have to learn to mask his thoughts, but that would be a skill he would hopefully learn in time. Or at least he would hopefully learn to choose representatives who could do it for him.

"I think he's starting to figure it out, Himeko," Daray said with a chuckle.

"If I truly want to change society, then I have to make sure that the disaffected groups have representation within my new government."

Tia's mouth twitched with a ghost of a smile as she heard Alaric's statement. The man may be a bit dense, but once he made a choice, he stuck to it.

"That is a start," Himeko stated. "You also need to think about what you can contribute on a bigger scale than just Polax. Even if you win the war, you will need to maintain relationships with your allies. You have to contribute to the greater society."

"You also need to prove yourself an effective leader and an effective government, otherwise your allies may decide that it is more efficient to take over rather than support you." Daray's frankness startled Alaric.

"You mean that Vukas would take over?" Tia interjected.

Himeko nodded. "The other planets in the galaxy can't afford for this sector to completely destabilize. It would mean that the war here would spill over into other civilizations. Most have allowed the Polaxian slave trade to continue, not because they support slavery, but because it kept this world stable. You are about to upset that balance, and if the rebels can't stabilize this area, then others are going to step in who can."

"They would betray us like that?" Tia was showing just how green she was in the realm of politics. Passion was a good thing to have, but a good diplomat also had to be pragmatic.

"Consider this another lesson in diplomacy." Himeko's eyes shifted between Tia and Alaric. "It is not a matter of betrayal. The leaders of other governments have their own interests that will always come first. In the good governments, those interests revolve around the well-being of their people. If your inexperience threatens that then they will step in not because they want to betray you but for the sake of their own people."

Daray joined the discussion, "They will give you a chance to do what needs to be done if you win the war, but their patience is not infinite."

"We have to win the war first," Alaric sighed.

"You do," Himeko agreed. "And the bulk of that battle is going to fall to you and the rest of the rebels." Himeko raised her hand to stop Alaric's protest. "I'm not saying that Vukas as an ally would not lend manpower or firepower, but we would not be here to fight your war for you." Himeko sighed. "Honestly, Alaric, you have done your people a disservice by not preparing them for this eventuality."

"I'm starting to see that," Alaric sighed.

Tia cleared her throat and the other three turned towards her.

"Um, while I don't know what was happening in the main city, I have had our people training for quite a while now. I also encouraged the other smaller city to do the same." Tia shifted slightly under their scrutiny, but she held her head high. "We all knew that at some point we were going to have to fight, whether it was attacking the enemy or defending ourselves from them. It didn't make any sense not to be prepared."

Daray laughed and clapped Alaric on the back as he stared at Tia. "If you don't make her your second in command then you are a fool."

Himeko ignored the antics of the men as Alaric shoved Daray. They didn't have time for the rituals of male bonding. They were heading to the surface tomorrow and they still had to figure out a way to survive until Reijo could get there.

"What kind of training?" Himeko demanded.

Tia shrugged, "Mostly in the use of various weapons. Even the children can fire a gun if necessary."

The men fell silent to listen to Tia and Himeko's discussion.

"Any other training?" Himeko prodded.

Tia looked to Alaric, who gave her a subtle nod. "I knew that we would be outnumbered and their weapons are better than what we have. So I have trained some small groups who specialize in guerilla warfare. I thought having teams that could get in and inflict as much damage as possible then disappear would be an effective strategy. A slave that works aboard one of the slavers has been passing me information about certain slaves. We have specifically targeted retrieval of a few because they were known to have skills as warriors or assassins."

"That was how you knew about Listar taking the Vukasin diplomat," Alaric exclaimed.

Tia nodded, "Your base was closer to his territory, which is why I passed the information along."

Himeko smiled. "You were already planning for the long game. Well done."

"You did all of this behind my back." Alaric sighed. "Why didn't you come to me?"

"I tried and you repeatedly dismissed me. You didn't want to hear from anyone else." Tia reached for Alaric's hand at his dejected look. "Everyone in these bases respects you and owes you for rescuing them, Alaric. But you have been sheltered. You have lived your life in relative safety here in the underwater cities. We have not. Every one of us knew that the peace here was fleeting."

"I have been a fool." Alaric removed his hand from Tia's and laid his head in his palms.

"You are only a fool if you don't learn from this, Alaric," Himeko chided. "We don't have time for self-pity. We need to come up with a plan for survival. It will be several days before the Vukasin fleet will make it to Polax. The battle will start long before that."

CHAPTER TWENTY-SIX

The transition to the surface over the next two days went surprisingly smooth. Tia proved herself to be a capable leader and organizational expert. She had everything coordinated with the other remaining underwater city and supplies, and people started arriving in waves to the stronghold the scouting party had found.

They still hadn't heard from the members of the scouting party since their last transmission. Daray regretted that he hadn't had a chance to clear the air with his childhood friend. He knew that Raylan was a skilled warrior. He hoped that was enough to bring his friend home.

Daray continued his inspection of their

stronghold. It was carved into the side of a mountain. The outer walls were thick stone and only on the front of the facility. The rest was built into the mountain itself. It looked as if this had been an ancient settlement of some sort, as they had to improvise ways to get energy to various rooms for illumination. Fortunately, the underwater cities had a multitude of portable energy devices, which only made sense considering.

Despite some crumbling along the outer walls, it was actually a very defensible position. The walls sloped down to a nearby beach, so a frontal assault would be easily seen. The mountain itself would provide cover from aerial attacks. Despite small numbers, Daray was feeling better about them being able to last until Reijo arrived. Himeko was at the moment setting up communications with a couple of the rebel techs. She would then transmit their location to Reijo using the Morse code she had used when she had been captured by the Polaxians. Even if the message were intercepted, the Polaxians wouldn't be able to decipher it.

Daray missed Himeko's presence, but he had his own work that he needed to accomplish.

Do you have need of me, my love?

Himeko's voice whispered through Daray's mind. Their bond was growing stronger by the minute. He was touched that she reached out to him when he missed her. It warmed his heart to know that she cared enough to do that.

I was just missing you, jinaria mio. You know the world loses its beauty when you ae not beside me.

He could feel the flush of warmth that enveloped both her mind and his. She wasn't used to such compliments, but she would be if he had any say in the matter.

I love you, Daray.

I love you too, Princess. I'm going back to work. You do the same. Maybe if we finish quickly we could....

He sent her erotic images of the two of them together. The last thing he heard in his mind was her gentle laughter as she closed the connection assured that he didn't need her; he just wanted her.

With a sigh, Daray moved towards the beach. They had already moved the weaponry for the people to carry. Today they were off loading the large-caliber weapons to counter any aerial or heavy machine attacks.

Many of the guns and such the rebels were carrying were old-fashioned projectile weapons— still deadly, but limited to firing only as long as they had ammunition. They had whole rooms stocked with ammunition, but he honestly didn't know how long that would last during a full-scale assault. So many unknowns had him nervous.

One unknown for him was the heavy weapons. All of the heavy weapons had been housed in the other underwater city, so today would be the first day that Daray would actually get to see what their full resources looked like.

He could hear Tia shouting orders as he hit the beach. Around the corner, he spotted a mass of men unloading huge crates from the massive cargo submarine that had surfaced further out in deeper waters.

An operation like this would have been simple for a Vukasin military unit. Anti-grav modules were standard issue for the Vukasin military. The rebels didn't have such devices, it seemed, because they were using archaic cranes and pullies to lift crates from the ship and placing them on flat-bottomed barges. The barges then ferried the equipment to the shore, where manpower and another set of pullies moved the cargo to waiting magnet sleds.

Daray was impressed at how smooth the operation was going even using such old-fashioned methods. It was humbling in a way. Himeko had often told him that technology wasn't a measure of capability. He was witnessing with his own eyes exactly what she meant. Daray wondered if he would have done half as well with the limited resources as the rebels had.

"Tia!" Daray raised a hand in greeting as he jogged down to the rocky shore.

Tia reached out and shook Daray's hand. "Good timing. This is the last of the weapons cargo to unload. After this we just have a few crates of food and medicine left."

She was handing the data pad to Daray when shouts from the cargo sub had her activating her comm to see what was going on.

"*Frexing* hell!" Tia growled before shouting orders to the men on the shore to double-time the off load.

"What's going on?" Daray asked.

"Communication from the underwater city suddenly stopped. They had royal ships circling above them for the last day or so, but we had thought that we had successfully masked their presence from the scans since they just circled."

Himeko?

I know, Daray. The royal forces located the underwater city. It was destroyed...no survivors.

Five hells! Cargo subs have been coming and going all day from that location. Why weren't we told that the royal ships had been circling overhead?

They told me that the rebel leaders thought they had it handled.

Not good enough. Full disclosure or no cooperation.

Daray felt a snort in his mind. *Just what do you think I am doing? Leave me alone and let me do my job. You get them ready for an attack.*

You're right. We have to assume that the ruling family knows where we are now.

"Get those damn guns into position!" Daray called to the crews.

"Hey!" Tia frowned at Daray with hands on her hips.

"We don't have time for power struggles, Tia. The government destroyed the underwater city. We have to assume that the royal family knows our location. It's time to get ready for war."

At his words, Tia looked as if she wanted to know how he knew the underwater city had been destroyed but instead started shouting orders to the men, urging them to get things done quickly. She commed the crew of the cargo sub and told them to pull into the deep-water cave connected to the stronghold. Those men couldn't go back to the destroyed city, so they were added to the personnel here.

Amazingly it didn't take long for all the cargo to be moved to the stronghold. Daray had hoped to inspect the weapons before their placement, but circumstances didn't allow for it. He let Tia get the equipment positioned. They had already discussed the best placement for what they had anticipated they were going to have. They lost about half a dozen of the anti-aerial assault weapons, so Daray shifted placement to try and cover the holes in their defenses. It wasn't perfect, but it would do if the weapons they had covered at least the smallest area that a Vukasin high-caliber weapon would cover.

They didn't have time for guesswork. Daray needed to see exactly what they had. He headed to the top of the outer wall. They were placing several guns across the wall so they could use them against both aerial and ground forces.

As Daray climbed the stairs to the platform at the top of the wall, his heart dropped. It couldn't be…this was their large weaponry? Electromagnetic pulse guns? Those things were practically ancient tech. Even the most basic species in the galaxy had already learned how to shield their equipment from EMP charges. If this was all they had, they were doomed.

"This is your heavy weaponry?!" He charged Tia, who was inspecting the installation. "You should have told me this was all you have. We would have come up with a different defense strategy. Damn it, you rebels are going to end up getting us all killed if you don't start being honest about things."

"Things are not as you think they are, *kijani*."

Daray spun around to confront the unfamiliar voice. He came face to face with a man who was obviously Vukasin. Then his eyes fell to the crest on his chest that carried the shesha serpent of the Tanis clan.

"Tanis," Daray growled. He attacked the man. The rebels had evidently sold them out to the Tanis.

Oddly enough, the man didn't retaliate or try to defend himself. He just stood there as Daray tackled him to the ground. It took Tia and three other rebels to peel Daray off of the Tanis man. They held him restrained while Tia tried to calm him down.

Daray?

We have been betrayed! The Tanis are in the compound.

I am seeing your memories, my love. He may be Tanis but his actions don't make sense. I can feel the same questions in your mind. Perhaps you should listen to why he is here.

I will not let the Tanis take you.

I'm not suggesting you should. You can both listen and be wary.

252

The fight left Daray's body. Himeko was right.

"Are you ready to listen?" Tia demanded.

"Yes," Daray growled.

She kept a wary eye on Daray but signaled for the men to release him. Daray jerked his arms away and crossed them over his chest. He glared at the Tanis man but made no move to attack him again.

"Are you alright, Dalir?" Tia asked the Tanis man, brushing the dust off his clothes as he stood up.

The man gave Tia a slight smile. "Nothing hurt but my pride." His face turned serious as he turned his eyes on Daray. "I understand your actions, Daray of the Nardo. I am Dalir, formerly of the Tanis."

"Formerly?" Daray questioned.

"It's a long story, but the short version of it is I was a slave that these people rescued." Dalir sighed and ran a hand through his hair.

Daray frowned at Tia. "Just because he was rescued as a slave doesn't mean that he isn't an enemy spy planted here."

Tia growled at Daray, "Do you think I am stupid? Alaric may be the idealist, but I lived and suffered in reality. I know that one you called friend could stab you in the back if it meant furthering their own cause. This man had to earn my trust before I would even let him out of his quarters."

There was a story in that outburst but Daray was more concerned with knowing the Tanis's story at the moment.

Dalir chuckled. "It's true. I spent a month in confinement while she investigated me and then another month working only with direct supervision."

"Why are you here, Tanis?" Daray leveled a look on him.

"I would appreciate if you called me Dalir. I renounced my connection to the Tanis a long time ago."

"Then why wear their insignia?" Daray still couldn't look on the Tanis crest without getting angry.

"Because unlike some people," Dalir gave

Tia a look and she bent her head away, not looking him in the eye, "I didn't want to deceive you about my origins. If I had and you discovered it was a lie later then I would never be trustworthy."

Daray had to give grudging respect to the man because what he says is true. "Fair enough."

"As to what I am doing here…. I am the rebel's weapons master."

CHAPTER TWENTY-SEVEN

Daray stared down Dalir. To his credit, the man didn't cringe or avert his eyes. His gaze remained steady. Old prejudices were difficult to overcome. Finally, Daray sighed.

"Look, I can't honestly say that I trust you."

Dalir shrugged as if this wasn't the first time he had faced this. "Fair enough."

Daray scowled at his easy acceptance of that. "I'm willing to give you a chance, however. But I need to know how you ended up here."

"I will tell you my history, but first you need to know what these weapons are capable of so you can plan how best to use them."

"I know what an electromagnetic pulse gun can do."

Dalir gave a small smile as he patted the barrel of the old pulse gun. "If this was the typical EMP gun, I wouldn't doubt that you do. You have to be very knowledgeable of what weapons can do if you are going to lead men in battle, and every Vukasin clan leader is expected to go to battle if called."

Daray was getting annoyed at Dalir's scholarly tone. He didn't need to be taught what his responsibilities were.

"Clan members are trained to answer their leaders call, just as you were trained to lead. But that is for a later conversation." Dalir walked around to the other side of the weapon. "This gun on the outside still looks like an EMP weapon. However, I have modified the functions of this weapon."

That piqued Daray's curiosity. "Modified how?"

"Depends on the specific gun. Though when we placed them I tried to direct the different modifications to be paired together so all functions are available for an area of defense." Dalir patted the gun in front of him. "For example, this one has been modified to disrupt the shielding most modern vessels now carry, allowing the electromagnetic pulse through to disrupt their systems. Unfortunately, it needs a rather large target to work, so the stun and pulse guns the soldiers carry won't be affected."

"While it means more bloodshed, we do have projectile weapons to counter soldiers on foot," Daray conceded.

Dalir nodded. "For the most part, this gun is for defensive purposes. Now that one," Dalir pointed to the gun positioned diagonally from the other weapon, "is designed to be an offensive weapon."

Curious, Daray asked, "What does it do?"

"It would be easier to show you than explain it."

"Make what preparations you need to demonstrate it. I want the rest of the commanders to see this as well. Would half an hour be enough time?" Daray waited until Dalir nodded his assent. "Tia, get the rest of the commanders here in that time. I will go get Himeko and Alaric."

Tia saluted and trotted off to find and gather the rest of the military commanders.

Daray turned to leave. He tossed over his shoulder, "Use the personnel here to get your demonstration set up. After the demonstration, I want your account of how you ended up here."

*****

A little before the half hour was up, Himeko was standing on the top of the highest wall with Daray and several other men. She studied the man Dalir. Daray had told her of his reservations about having someone from the Tanis clan in such an important position. She also knew that accidents of birth didn't necessarily dictate what kind of man you were. It was a gamble in a time of war, but she was willing to reserve judgement until she knew the man better.

"Gentlemen...ladies," Dalir addressed the assembled group. "I would like you to direct your attention to that large boulder halfway down the shoreline."

Himeko squinted into the setting sun. Once her eyes adjusted, she could make out the enormous rock Dalir had indicated. It was at least as tall as the stronghold's first wall and almost as wide. It would take several teams of men and heavy equipment to move such a stone.

Daray nodded to Dalir to continue. The man flipped a few switches on the weapon and the air around them changed. The hair on Himeko's arms stood up and she felt almost like she was standing next to a Tesla coil. The air around them was charged, but it somehow felt different from anything she had experienced before. As the weapons charged up, her head buzzed as if it were filled with a hive of bees. It became almost painful, and Himeko had to fight to keep from shutting her eyes against the noise. Instinctively she covered her ears, though that did nothing for the chaos in her head.

The weapon fired and the pressure in her skull instantly lessened. Their eyes remained glued to the large stone on the shore. They watched in horror as the stone seemed to disappear like ash falling away from a burning branch.

"Five hells!" Daray gasped next to her.

She could feel his shock through their connection. Even through the shock she could see his mind planning. This was a shock and awe weapon. It was meant to be used as either a last resort or a preemptive strike to kill the moral of the opposing force. It was the kind of weapon of mass destruction that she would normally advocate treaties be created to control their existence and use.

Despite her kneejerk moral objection to such a weapon, the pragmatic side of her knew it may be the one thing that kept them alive long enough for the Vukasin forces to come to their aide.

The way the weapon disintegrated the rock outcropping until nothing was left stirred a memory in Himeko's mind. Then it clicked...the briefings from Banji and Aki.

"Dalir, is this weapon's modifications based off the Tanis gun that disintegrates its victims that we have been seeing lately?" Himeko asked.

Dalir looked surprised. "I hadn't heard that they put those into combat situations." He looked between his weapon and Himeko. "I worked on the prototype of the other weapon. This one works on similar principles."

"You made that damn weapon?" Daray's fists clenched as he growled out the question. "Do you have any idea how many people have died because of that thing?"

Himeko laid a restraining hand on her mate's arm.

Daray, your anger won't do any good at this moment. I can see the memories that are in the forefront of your mind. I understand the horror at what you saw.

They screamed, Himeko...until they disappeared they screamed.

Walk away for a bit, my love. Let me handle the rest.

Bring him to the conference room. I have to know his story. I don't trust him.

Daray stalked away and Himeko turned back to Dalir, who had a shocked look on his face.

"I figured the other Vukasins would have trust issues with me because I was born in the Tanis clan, but I never expected to be outright hated," Dalir sighed.

Himeko dismiss the rest of the men since the demonstration was over. Dalir, Alaric, and Tia were the only ones who remained with Himeko.

"He doesn't hate you, but this weapon of

yours has brought up some very traumatic memories," Himeko said quietly. "He saw firsthand what it is capable of and it haunts him."

The group fell into silence. There was nothing anyone could say about the horrors of war.

"I want these weapons to be rigged to be destroyed at a moment's notice." Alaric broke the silence hanging over them.

"What? Why?" Tia asked.

"Do you want the enemy to have this technology?" Alaric demanded.

Himeko could tell that neither Tia nor Dalir had thought about that. She was impressed that Alaric had considered a scenario where they might have to abandon the stronghold. Perhaps there was hope for the young Polaxian royal yet.

"Alaric is right. A weapon such as this in the hands of an enemy without conscience would be devastating. We have to consider the possibility that we will be defeated or forced to retreat. Would you want this weapon turned on your friends and family?"

Himeko patiently schooled the inexperienced

Tia and the scholar Dalir. She had dealt with many academics over the years; they often tended to think strictly in "can this be done" lines of thought instead of "should this be done." Dalir didn't seem to be any different. It didn't inherently make him a bad man. Himeko did wonder if Dalir had his own moral limits or if he would be one of those scientists that require a handler for moral guidance.

She saw Tia get the implications almost immediately. It took Dalir a little longer.

"I hadn't thought of that," Dalir sighed. "I only thought of it as a way to protect those I care about."

"You must remember in war, Dalir, that if you can use something against your enemy then they can use it against you. If we use that weapon against those attacking us, I can guarantee that the Tanis will start working on their own versions of the weapon. They may not have thought to use it in such a large scale as you did, but if they see it they will."

"I need to start working on a defense."

Himeko could see Dalir's mind disappearing into scientific thought. She stopped him as he absently started moving away.

"Daray needs to speak with you. Come with me please."

Dalir paled little, remembering Daray's face twisted with anger before he had left. But he followed after Himeko.

CHAPTER TWENTY-EIGHT

They entered the conference room to see Daray sitting at the table with his head in his hands. He looked up as Himeko and Dalir entered. He gave a slight smile to his mate, but Daray's eyes look haunted when he turned them on Dalir.

Daray motioned for the weapons master to sit. "I'm going to be honest, I am not sure that I will ever trust you. But you are here now and I have to know how that came to be."

Dalir sat across from the Vukasin pair.

"It is a long story."

"I still need to know," said Daray.

"It starts long before the women of Earth came to Vukas. Our clan leader, Bel, had already started grooming the clan members for revolt. Within the Tanis territories, propaganda was rampant. The loss of our women, the lack of resources for poorer families…all of it was laid at Ivalio's feet."

Daray nodded but said nothing. He wasn't surprised to hear what Dalir was saying. The more they had delved into the Tanis affairs the clearer it became that their treachery was a long time in the making.

Himeko asked, "Did you know that it was a Tanis who created the virus that caused the loss of your women?"

Dalir seemed shocked at first and shook his head to deny it. His face then turned thoughtful and he sighed.

Dalir continued, "Early on, Bel sponsored the clan scientists to work on whatever interested them. It was a euphoric state for an academic. But as time passed, the credits quickly shifted to only certain lines of study…basically only things that could be weaponized. I was among a group that studied how to harness certain energies and discharge them at will. Originally we were wanting to find a way to better store energy for household use. It wasn't until a laboratory accident occurred that the possibility of weapons applications even crossed our minds."

Dalir looked off into space as he remembered. "My colleague…no, my friend, died in that accident. Bel's liaison then pushed for us to study what happened and how to replicate the accident at will. He claimed we had to know for safety reasons.

By this time the Earth women had arrived and there was a certain sense of urgency to the higher ups within the clan. It didn't take long before they were demanding we turn our research towards weapons applications. They made it sound like we were attacked without cause. It would be almost a year before I started to question Bel and his policies."

"Why did it take you so long? I mean conquering entire planets, the slave trade…five hells! The treason against your *Khalon*…none of that made you wonder?" Daray demanded, slamming his fist on the conference table.

Dalir jumped slightly at the noise but he looked Daray in the eye. "You have to understand;

clan members are taught loyalty to the clan above all else from the moment of their birth. Honestly, most of the clan knew nothing of any of that. We were told that our clan was attacked and we had to defend ourselves. Until most of the clan was forced to leave Vukas, the everyday people had no idea what the clan leaders were doing.

I knew nothing of those things until I was a scientist assigned to Ludus Prime. The slavery disgusted me, but many of my fellow Tanis gave in to their baser selves and convinced themselves that if they weren't Tanis then they weren't truly people, just tools to be used. Evil will flourish if given half a chance. Imagine what evil does when given free reign."

That statement seemed to deflate Daray's righteous anger somewhat.

"As one man there wasn't much I could do. I delayed research, sabotaged small things here and there, but if I drew too much notice to myself then it was over for me as well."

"If you didn't draw notice to yourself, how did you end up as a slave?" Himeko quietly asked.

Dalir sighed. "Every man has his limits…"

"What was yours?" Daray asked quietly. He still didn't fully trust this Tanis, but he knew that accident of clan birth didn't make you a bad man; there were several former Tanis that had cut ties with their clan after Bel's assassination attempt of Megan. But this man had worked for the Tanis long after that. It was possible that those actually in Tanis territory hadn't heard what really had happened.

This was easier when I didn't have any doubts.

But it shows you are a good man because you won't condemn someone for something they had no power over.

Daray felt Himeko's fingers caress his face in his mind. By the gods, he loved that woman.

"I had been assigned to a group to design new slave collars. We scientists and engineers no longer had a choice in what projects we worked on. You went where you were told or you were arrested for crimes against the clan. Bel was tired of the Ludus people and the women stolen from Earth organizing resistance. The old slave collars had punishment devices worked into them. They were painful, even torturous on their highest settings, but none lethal. Too many of the slaves valued their

270

freedom more than they feared the pain. So, he ordered a lethal collar to be constructed. One that could still be used as punishment without inflicting death, but one that could also deliver death even when the one with the controls was at a distance. But he didn't want just a death; he was a gruesome, spectacular death.

"I tried to sabotage the workings to slow down its production, but in reality it was a simple process to combine the original collar with an explosive device. I couldn't stop it from being made."

Dalir stopped talking and lowered his head to study his hands. The seconds ticked away with him not continuing his story. Himeko noticed that Dalir's shoulders were shaking and then she and Daray heard the man sniff. He was quietly crying.

Himeko reached over and laid her small hand on Dalir's clasped hands. She said softly, "I'm sorry, Dalir, but we need to hear the rest."

Dalir raised his head to look her in the eyes. He saw regret and compassion there.

Dalir sniffed and wiped his face with the sleeve of his shirt. "I'm going to be honest. I try not to think about this next part too much."

Even Daray nodded his understanding.

Dalir heaved a steadying breath and then started to speak again. "We tested those collars separate from living subjects. We used the deceased to measure the damage it would cause to flesh and bone until the explosion destroyed the head in its entirety just as ordered. The idea that this device that I had been forced to work on could so casually end a life made me sick to my stomach.

When we informed our liaison that we were finished, Bel himself came to see the final product. He wanted a demonstration of its effectiveness. I went to prepare one of the corpses we had in storage for the demonstration only to be stopped by Bel's security detail. He wanted to see its effects on a live subject."

Dalir visibly shuttered at the memory.

"They pulled a pretty little Ludus Prime female to the center of the test space. They lined up several other slaves around the perimeter. I later found out that the female had successfully fought off one of the guards when he tried to rape her. The people lined up around the perimeter were the men who came to her defense and her family. Five hells!" Dalir broke down and sobbed into his hands, "They brought in her children…her children…."

Dalir straightened, and for the first time Daray and Himeko saw anger and hatred twist his features.

"In that moment, any hope I had that the Tanis would one day wake up from the hell they were creating died. Bel was nothing but pure evil."

"Tell us the rest, Dalir," Daray quietly urged.

"I was ordered to collar the poor woman and bring the remote device to Bel. I refused." Dalir swallowed back fresh tears. "Not that my act of defiance did that poor woman any good. Someone else followed the orders I wasn't willing to. I can still see her children crying covered in the gore that was once their mother. I honestly don't know what happened to the rest of those people because I rushed Bel in a rage. I didn't make it anywhere close to him, as his guards caught me and beat me nearly to death before dragging me away.

My sentence was to have my mind destroyed and be sold off as slave labor. So at least I would profit the Tanis clan somehow."

Daray frowned. "Your mind is obviously fine…. I don't see Bel changing his mind once he makes that kind of decision."

"You're right," Dalir conceded. "I am only whole because the technician assigned to carry out destroying my mind was a friend of mine. He purposely misplaced the probes to inflict minimum damage. Still hurt like the pit of the five hells, so Bel and his cronies saw exactly what they wanted to during the procedure. It also rendered me a blathering idiot for a few hours, but I was able to recover with the only lasting damage being a nerve tick that gets worse as I am stressed.

I spent several months doing mindless manual labor until I was sold again to a Polaxian slaver. When I was brought to this planet for cataloguing and processing, the rebels saved me."

"You have given me a lot to think about, Dalir." Daray stood, indicting that he had heard enough. "I'm sorry I made you relive those memories."

Daray extended his hand towards Dalir. Dalir looked a little shocked but he took Daray's hand with a wry smile.

"I can't say that I wouldn't have done the same in your shoes. Now if you will excuse me. I have a few ideas about shielding against the disintegration gun.

CHAPTER TWENTY-NINE

Himeko and Daray stood as Dalir exited the room. Daray gave Himeko a wolfish grin and stalked her around the table.

Himeko giggled but held her hands up to ward him off. "We still have a lot of work to do today."

Daray grabbed her around the waist and leaned in to nibble on her neck as she playfully shoved at him and giggled. "But I haven't seen you all day, *jinaria mio*." He let out a sigh and said mournfully, "Besides, I need something beautiful after hearing his story."

He kissed her neck and sucked at the spot

that sported his mating bite. Himeko moaned and melted into his embrace. She had missed him today too. Of course, she wouldn't admit it out load because the man would take it as an invitation.

I can read your mind, my princess. I don't need an invitation to want you. You just have to walk into my presence or flit through my mind and I am hard and willing.

Himeko's entire body flushed as Daray's declaration filled her mind. There was such a strong ring of truth to it, an absolute that she hadn't thought possible. After being with Daray, she knew that she would never have been happy in an arranged marriage that didn't contain love and passion.

"Just so you know it is bad form to think about other men, even in the abstract, when your mate is trying to seduce you." Daray nipped her ear and then suckled the sting away.

Himeko turned in his arms and caressed his cheek before kissing him deeply. She poured all of her love and the epiphany she just realized into that kiss.

Daray chuckled against her lips and pulled her in close. "Well I suppose I can forgive you if you kiss me like that again." He reached down and adjusted himself. "But wait until I get you alone in our quarters."

Daray scooped her up into his arms and stated carrying her towards the door. He was about to reach for the door when it crashed open.

Standing before them, grinning malevolently, was Listar.

Daray put Himeko down and pushed her slightly behind him to protect her. Himeko reached for the *tessen* she kept on her person at all times now.

"How in the five hells did you get in here?" Daray demanded.

Listar advanced towards the pair. "I have come to retrieve my property."

"I am no man's property," Himeko declared.

Listar laughed until Daray sent a strong upper cut into his midsection. Listar's laugh turned into a groan as he doubled over slightly.

"You'll pay for that, Vukasin. I was going to let you live since you are so close to the royal family, Nardo clan head, because my father doesn't want war with Vukas just yet. But accidents do happen. He even demanded that we not bring energy weapons so there weren't any 'accidents.' However, I have no qualms about watching you be torn limb from limb."

A full contingent of Polaxian soldiers poured into the tight confines of the room they had been using as a conference room. Daray shifted as the men closed in on him and Himeko. He would not let them take her. Himeko placed her back against Daray's and opened her war fan.

I am with you, my love.

Eternity filled a single moment as time stopped. Circled around them was their doom, but they would go down together knowing that their friends would exact justice for their deaths. It amazed Himeko how calm she could be in the face of her death. She had lived a life that held no regrets. All that was left was to die well and with honor.

Almost as if they were one person, Daray and Himeko burst into action. They easily wiped out the first line of the enemy. Himeko's *tessen* whistled through the air, slicing major arteries until a fountain of blood surrounded her. Daray had phased into his battle beast and gave over to the primal instinct to protect his mate. Tooth and claw tore at his enemy until Daray was covered in gore.

Listar screamed obscenities at his men as they hesitated against the brutality of the normally stoic pair. The ignorant soldiers now understood that quiet calm wasn't weakness but rather a tight control on deadly skills.

Listar pushed his men forward. "Attack them together and overwhelm them! You are Polaxians, failure is dishonor!"

Galvanized by their leader's words, the soldiers attacked en mass. Even with the enemy slipping in the blood of their comrades, sheer numbers finally overwhelmed the pair. Himeko's war fan lodged in the chest of the Polaxian that suddenly rushed her. Without a weapon, the amount of damage she could inflict on men twice her size was limited, especially since they crowded around her, making movement difficult. It wasn't long before a pair of soldiers had her trapped and were carting her away.

Daray!

Daray turned to see his mate struggling against two men as she was carried away from him. He vaguely heard Listar call to him men not to kill Himeko because their buyer wanted her alive. Daray lost all control of his primal side. He tore a bloody path to get to Himeko. Unfortunately, his single-minded determination ignored the fact that he was surrounded by the enemy.

One of the soldiers behind him landed a lucky blow with the club he carried. It hit Daray's battle collar that he had made sure was always on since they came to the stronghold. The blow rattled his head, but it shifted the collar just enough to hit the bundle of nerves that was a phased Vukasin's weakness. His entire body spasmed and his joints locked. He watched helplessly as Himeko disappeared out the door and his body tumbled to the ground. He couldn't even roar out his frustration.

Suddenly alarms started blaring through the stronghold. Someone finally had discovered that the enemy had infiltrated their ranks.

"Finish him!" Listar growled.

Daray eyes trailed the path of the club as it descended towards his head. A blinding pain and then nothing.

CHAPTER THIRTY

"Daray…Daray."

His head throbbed each time his name was called. He couldn't be dead; he was in too much pain. Daray gingerly opened his eyes; the bright lights sent a fresh stab of pain through his head. For a brief moment he wondered how he had gotten into this position. Then he remembered Listar's attack and Himeko being dragged away.

Daray bolted upright only to lean over the med-bed to empty the contents of his stomach all over the floor. Hands pushed him back against the bed and he let them.

"Easy there. The medics say you have a

really nasty concussion."

Daray cracked his eyes and saw his old friend Raylan standing over him.

"Himeko?" Daray groaned.

"We'll get her back." Raylan sighed. "I'm sorry I didn't make it back in time to warn you."

"Warn me?"

Raylan opened his mouth to answer only to be interrupted when the head medic called out to them.

"We're ready for him."

Raylan stood up to make room for the other medics to get around the mess that Daray had made. Two orderlies were already mopping up the mess.

"Listen…they are going to send you through a regen treatment so you will be in top condition for the coming battle. We will talk when you are done."

Raylan walked away even as Daray tried to reach out and grab him. He didn't want to waste time with treatment. He wanted to leave now. But when his world spun out of control with his movement, Daray had to concede that perhaps treatment was necessary.

A couple of hours later, Daray and Raylan were in the conference room with Alaric.

"Someone betrayed us!" Daray growled. His gut reaction was Dalir was a Tanis plant, but when Daray had tracked him down he found out that the man hadn't left the lab and had been tirelessly creating a shield that disperses the effects of the disintegrating weapon. The prototype he had created only worked to cover a single person, but he already had the other engineers creating as many units as possible in a short amount of time. Dalir was also trying to modify a few of the shields found on the walls to protect those without individual shields. As much as Daray wanted a target for his rage, he had to concede that at this point Dalir didn't seem to be the logical choice.

"It was Dorax," Raylan said.

"Dorax?!" Alaric jumped up, slamming his fist on the table. "That's not possible; he has been my friend since we were children."

"I doubt he wanted to betray you," Raylan sighed. "He was captured. We tried to get him back, but they publicly executed him. It was obvious he had been tortured." Raylan fell silent, his eyes shut against the memories. "Just before they fired upon him with one of those new disintegrating guns the Tanis have started favoring, he yelled out 'protect the rebels.' I can still hear his screams as he died."

"That doesn't explain how Listar and his men made it into the stronghold without any of us knowing until it was too late." Daray didn't have time for Alaric to wallow in his grief at betrayal. Daray felt that in some ways it was his own fault for not fully preparing the rebels for the horrors of war.

Raylan slid a data pad over to Daray.

"This does."

Daray activated the pad and a schematic of the stronghold popped up. The plans even showed several hidden entrances and exits that the rebels hadn't even discovered yet.

"Get men in these areas," Daray demanded.

"Already done," Raylan answered.

Daray pushed the data pad over to Alaric.

"Where did they get this?" Alaric asked as he

handed the pad back to Raylan.

"Royal archive." Raylan took the pad and shut it down. "I took this off a dead Polaxian soldier. It would seem that Listar had them comb through documents once he tortured the location out of Dorax. This was one of several old military outposts that had been abandoned a few generations ago. Much like the underwater cities, except the slaves hadn't wiped the existence of the outposts from the archives."

"So you are saying that our enemy has plans to our safe haven?" Alaric growled.

"They do."

"How are we supposed to keep our people safe then?" Alaric was beginning to realize just how much the odds were against the rebels succeeding.

"We analyze weak points, just like they would. We anticipate what the enemy may do and take measures to counter attack. We create several fortification points that we can defend if we have to fall back. We survive until reinforcements get here." Daray already had several battle plans forming in his mind. The main question was, would Alaric be strong enough to lead in the heat of battle because

Daray wasn't going to be there. He was going after his mate. "Raylan, did you contact Reijo?"

"I did. His ship and two others are heading our way at maximum speed. They should be here within twenty-six hours. The rest of the force will arrive a day after that."

"Tia!" Daray bellowed.

Just as he figured, the woman popped her head through the door. She was inexperienced but she was smart and determined. She may be the person Alaric needed to keep it together in battle.

Daray nodded at the woman, then directed his comments to her and Alaric both. "Get the people armed. Move the children deeper into the stronghold to a secure location. Everyone capable of carrying a weapon needs—"

"Alaric!" a panicked voice came over the comm.

"What is it, Ludi?"

"There is an army unloading from ships along the shore!"

"Damn, I had hoped we would have a little

bit more time." Daray started sending messages to various teams throughout the stronghold.

"Dalir!" Daray called down to the lab. "Dalir!"

"Oh sorry, I was in the middle of a fascinating reaction…." Dalir's voice finally filtered across the comm.

"Later, Dalir. The enemy is at our door. How are the shields coming?"

"The highest wall is covered, but that is it at the moment."

"What about our shock and awe weapon?"

"Six are operational. All have been rigged to be destroyed if necessary."

It wasn't as good as he had hoped, but it was at least something. He looked up and saw that Tia and Alaric were still standing there.

"Let's get moving people," Daray shooed them out.

"Do you think they will survive without us?" Raylan asked after the rebel pair left.

"Us?"

"Do you really think that I am going to let you go after Himeko on your own?" Raylan shook his head. "I may not want her as a mate, but that doesn't mean I don't love her. She has become one of my closest friends as we traveled around the galaxy for diplomatic missions."

Daray nodded. "Um, about…." He shrugged and gestured towards the sea. "I'm sorry."

"I'm not," Raylan grinned. "If that was what it took to get your head out of your ass it was worth a few bruises."

"The rebels have to hold out for about a day before the cavalry comes to the rescue. With Reijo they can hold out until the rest of the forces get here. That shouldn't be a problem if they don't panic and play it smart."

Raylan's grinning face turned serious. "Then you need to hurry up and get those battle plans to the team leaders so we can go get our girl.".

CHAPTER THIRTY-ONE

Daray could feel that Himeko was still alive, but she remained stubbornly silent in the hours since she was taken. All he had was a sense of direction and he knew she couldn't be far because his connection to her was so strong.

"I haven't been able to vet the information, but it appears that Himeko is in the enemy camp," Raylan whispered to Daray. "At least for now."

"Sounds about right. I can feel her presence in that direction," Daray answered.

The pair were hidden among the boulders of the rocky shore. So far they had evaded the various patrols. All in all, the Polaxian military discipline was lackluster at best. They acted more like a bunch of mercenaries out to party and create carnage than an organized force.

It had been almost three hours since the last seafaring ship had deposited soldiers and supplies. The force was impressive, but not overwhelming. Daray wondered if they knew something the rebels didn't or if they were just underestimating the ragtag gathering of ex-slaves. He hoped it was the latter.

Raylan and Daray were slowly advancing towards the officers' area. Here, instead of tents they had erected temporary shells with climate control. Himeko was somewhere within that metal maze.

The two men were inching forward to find a good observation spot. The plan was to search the area under the cover of night.

Suddenly pain exploded in Daray's head. It was only years of discipline that kept him from giving away their position. He swallowed the cry of pain that wanted to erupt from his throat. His vision blurred.

This pain was not his own. He quickly closed off his connection to Himeko just long enough to clear his head so he could concentrate again. But he couldn't stay away more than a few moments.

What in the five hells was that, Himeko?

He could feel the throbbing pain she was experiencing through their connection, but she refused to talk to him.

Answer me! By the gods, I am going to phase and tear this whole camp apart to find you.

Daray could feel Himeko sigh in his mind.

And you wonder why I stayed silent. You need to stay in control, my love, not rage over my treatment.

What happened? Daray growled.

One of the Polaxian guards licked me. I didn't like it so I used my head to crash into his jaw. He bit the end of his tongue off.

Daray had to grin at her smug delight at causing the guard injury.

That doesn't explain the extreme pain I felt, jinaria.

Well, that was the other guard hitting me in

the face with the butt of a pulse rifle.

I'm going to tear them apart and mount their heads.

While your macho anger is sweet, please don't lose control. This whole situation is delicate and I need to be here a little longer to find out what is going on.

No! I'm getting you out of there as soon as possible.

Please, Daray...this is important.

Daray crushed the stone underneath his hands. He wanted to put his foot down and absolutely refuse Himeko in this, but he knew her well enough that she wouldn't subject herself to such indignities lightly. He had to trust that the information she was trying to gather was important.

Fine, but you keep our connection fully open at all times. No more trying to shield me. And, Himeko, if I think you are in immediate danger I am coming to get you no matter what.

Fair enough. If I haven't told you today, I love you.

I love you too, Princess.

"What did Himeko say?" Raylan watched his friend in concern. He could still see the anger and need to inflict harm for Himeko's sake in the tension of Daray's body. He knew that Daray knew exactly which structure Himeko was in but for some reason he was waiting to rescue her.

Daray didn't say anything. Instead he gestured for Raylan to follow him.

Raylan followed Daray, taking note of everything surrounding them and mapping a few escape routes. The Polaxians may have been worthy opponents in a space battle, but their camp set up made it fairly obvious they had little if any experience with a full-scale battle on terra firma. They had haphazardly set up the officers' shelters and there didn't seem to be a plan to the lighting. A few bonfires were dotted here and there and an artificial lamp only if the officer demanded one. Even a Vukasin cadet still in his den would know that a war camp should be set up in an orderly fashion with lighting placed to keep the enemy from having places of deep shadow like he and Daray now hid in.

Raylan took another look at his friend. Daray

used the signs that soldiers on Vukas were taught for silent communication., so Raylan knew that Himeko was in the structure directly across from their hiding place. He settled in to wait next to Daray. Raylan may not know what is going on, but he trusted Himeko and Daray.

*****

Himeko kept her connection open to Daray just as she promised, but she had enough mental discipline to slightly filter the information he received. Their connection made it impossible to outright lie to him, so she kept the connection only to her emotional state and physical sensations. She didn't want Daray to know that there were several Tanis representatives in Listar's temporary quarters where she was being held.

She loved Daray, and normally he was very calm and considered a problem from several angles before acting. He didn't seem to have the same patience when it came to her though. She couldn't have him crashing in to save her.

Her head was still ringing from the blow of the pulse rifle to her face. Already her left eye was swelling shut. She kept her head down and moaned once in a while to keep up the appearance of beaten captive. She already knew that Listar was trading her to the Tanis. If that had been all, she would have let Daray take her away from here already, but she had heard a snippet of conversation between Listar and the Tanis representative. She was evidently being traded for a weapon of some sort because Bel wanted to kill her personally for the insult of stabbing him.

"Are you sure that this will wipe out the rebels?" Listar's voice raised in excitement.

"I assure you, Lord Listar, that all of the experiments show a ninety-six percent kill rate. The few that would survive would be easily crushed."

That nasally voice must be the Tanis in charge here at the war camp.

"You have already infected the capital, correct?"

"As you ordered, the royal palace was the first to be infected. Already people are sickening and dying. You will be hailed as the savior of your people when you bring them the treatment. If any of your brothers survive, the people will still demand you are crowned in place of your father."

"How long before the poisoned water supply

wipes out the rebels?"

"In two more days, we should start seeing the first casualties."

"My intel says that the rebels have formed an alliance with the Vukasins…."

"Don't worry, it is just as lethal to my kind as it is to yours."

"You did bring the serum for me and my men?"

For the first time, Listar sounded slightly nervous. He may be willing to kill off his own people to obtain power, but he didn't want to be in danger of dying himself.

"Your men are being inoculated as we speak, and I brought your dose with me to administer."

"And the doses to take back to the capital?"

"Safely stored in the medical facility at the center of camp under guard. We will deliver the last of the payment once Bel arrives to take possession of the woman."

Daray! The Tanis have given a fast acting

lethal plague to Listar. He's planning on wiping out not only the rebels but the royal family as well. You have to get the treatment to Alaric or we are all dead, including Reijo and the rest of the Vukasins coming.

I'm not leaving you, Himeko.

Oh you damn stubborn man! This is bigger than just us. What do you think will happen to the entire galaxy if one of the infected make it off planet? It could be an epidemic of extinction proportions. We don't matter in the big scheme of things.

You will always matter to me, Himeko.

Himeko couldn't help the melting sensation around her heart. She knew that sacrificing herself for the good of many was necessary. He could either get the cure or he would free her, but he couldn't do both. She and Daray might be able to escape after one commotion, but the entire army would be ready if they tried to pull a second operation. Even knowing that, she still felt loved because of Daray's declaration. It was the first time in her life that she felt like someone put her first.

I love you, Daray. Please try to be happy for

me.

Himeko pushed the memories of what Listar and the Tanis had discussed. She was confident that Daray would ultimately do the right thing, even if he raged against having to make that decision. She then severed their connection.

CHAPTER THIRTY-TWO

Himeko! Himeko!

Daray pushed all of his mental power out into their connection trying to reconnect to his mate, but Himeko had as much if not more mental discipline as Daray and she kept him firmly shut out.

How could she ask this of him? How could she force him to decide between her and everyone else? Didn't she know that once she walked into his life no one else mattered anymore? Without her there was nothing in this universe worth living for as far as he was concerned.

Daray was so engulfed in his grief and rage that he hadn't paid attention to his surroundings.

When Raylan laid a hand on his shoulder, Daray was so startled that he turned swinging his fist. He stopped just millimeters from Raylan's jaw.

"What?" Daray growled at his friend.

"Judging by your face, Himeko told you something that you didn't want to hear. So when are we bursting in to rescue the princess?"

Daray's eyes shimmered with unshed tears and he clenched his teeth before his shoulders slumped with a sigh. "We're not. The mission has changed."

At Raylan's incredulous look, Daray explained what Himeko had overheard.

"I don't care! You get back into her head and you make her understand that leaving her behind is not an option." Raylan's frantic whispers we rising in volume. Both men were endangering either mission.

Daray took a deep breath. It was practically impossible, but he had to push aside his feelings for Himeko and think about the situation rationally. He understood that was why Himeko had cut off contact. He never would have been able to separate his feeling for her and it would compromise his ability to think objectively. He didn't have to like it, but he had to respect Himeko for it.

"Himeko's right. This plague is more important. One life sacrificed for the good of millions."

"I always knew you were a cold-blooded bastard…but she is your mate, Daray."

"You think I don't know that! That it isn't eating me up inside that I have to stand by and watch the one person I have ever truly loved in my entire life die to protect people I couldn't give dragon-spider shit about?" Daray's fierce rant ended as he took a steadying breath. "Himeko is the one who cares about the people. It is for her sake…." Daray swallowed a sob. He refused to cry. He had a job to do. He could fall apart afterwards.

Raylan punched Daray. "You are a *frexing* idiot." He grabbed Daray's shirt and dragged him close until they were nose to nose. "You aren't in this alone."

Daray's eyes opened wider. He was so used to doing everything that he had forgotten how to lean on his friends. Thank the gods that Raylan was there to remind him.

Daray nodded. "The medical facility is at the center of the camp. From what Himeko overheard, it sounds like it is probably heavily guarded. Are you sure that you can get in and out alone?"

Raylan gave his easy-going grin. "Of course, I'm going to use you and Himeko as a distraction after all."

Daray finally chuckled. Hope started to fill him up. Maybe, just maybe, that could rescue the princess and the planet both.

"Fine, but give us enough of a head start to actually get out of here."

Raylan reached into his pouch and pulled Himeko's battered war fan out. He pressed it into Daray's hands. "Get her out and I will get the plague cure."

Daray's fingers tightened around Himeko's *tessen*. It was just a hunk of metal and cloth, but somehow it made him feel closer to the woman who was still blocking him from her mind. He couldn't even tell her that he was coming for her.

He extended his hand towards the man who had been his childhood friend and then Himeko's protector on her diplomatic missions. He knew he owed Raylan more than he could ever repay.

Raylan gripped Daray's forearm in a warrior's handshake that would be a familiar sign of respect in almost any time or culture.

"Go with honor, my friend." Daray gave Raylan's arm an affectionate squeeze. "Come back safe or I will never hear the end of it from Himeko."

"You bring the princess home and I will take care of the rest." Raylan gave a wink. "And just so you know, when we get back to Vukas I am borrowing the vacation villa on the southern island."

"We get through this alive and well and I will give you the damned villa."

Daray pulled his friend back behind the boulder that had sheltered them as a soldier's patrol passed.

"If they hold to their pattern, we have about half an hour before another patrol goes through." Raylan nodded his agreement with Daray. "We meet back at the stronghold in three hours' time or less. If I am not back by then with Himeko, your priority it to get the people treated. If we make it back first, I will put the medics on isolating the disease and working towards a solution in case you don't make it back."

With a final handshake, the friends parted
ways. Now it was left up to fate and the gods of war
whether or not they were successful.

CHAPTER THIRTY-THREE

Himeko watched Listar as the Tanis medic, at least she assumed he was a medic, injected him with a thick golden liquid. Judging by Listar's wince, the injection hurt somewhat. The medic then raised a hand to his ear as if he were hearing someone on an ear piece. He leaned over and said something to Listar. Himeko couldn't hear what they said but both men moved out of the way.

Himeko felt the change in atmosphere and she knew that someone would soon be arriving by slip stream. Personal slip-stream tech was a new and costly development. The Tanis only allowed their highest officers and operatives to own the device. They had been fortunate to capture a few of the earlier models, and Ghaleb had the remaining scientists reverse engineer their own version of the device. Ghaleb had wanted all of his warriors and diplomats to carry one until it became clear that such a thing would be cost prohibitive. The royal house of Ivalio and the Vukasin government might have deep pockets when it came to credits, but they didn't have an unlimited supply.

The air around them compressed and then popped as an area in the center of the temporary structure wavered, like looking through the heat of a fire. Himeko opened her jaw, trying to pop her ears from the pressure change. For a moment, she wondered if anyone was going to come through the slip stream, as they usually appeared almost instantly. Little by little, Bel's corpulent figured appeared in the space before her.

The slip stream popped once more and disappeared as the vile man sneered down at the bound Himeko. Even in her battered state she raised her chin and glared at him defiantly.

Bel's eyes narrowed on the scar of the mating bite that showed through her torn clothing. He grabbed her shirt and drug her close. Himeko cringed as he buried his nose in her neck and inhaled deeply.

"I see the Nardo fool has claimed you. Good. Perhaps we can drive him mad as he feels our abuse of you, breeder."

Himeko did something she never would have imagined doing. She spit in Bel's face. The Tanis leader tossed her to the ground and kicked her side as he wiped the spittle from his face.

"You will pay for that, breeder." He sneered at her. "Perhaps I should let my guard soften you up before availing myself of your charms."

Himeko would kill herself before allowing the Tanis to subject her to repeated rapes.

Himeko sneered right back at Bel with a chuckle. "Of course you would have to send your men in to do the job. Tell me, can you even find your manhood within the rolls of fat that surround you?"

The Polaxians snickered as Bel's face turned nearly purple. Even the Tanis personnel had to cough to cover their own laughter.

Bel roared and kicked her again and again. She was helpless, with her hand bound behind her back and her ankles tied together. If she was lucky, Bel would beat her to death before any of the men were allowed to touch her. She didn't want any other man than Daray to touch her intimately.

Himeko felt one of her ribs crack and she couldn't keep from crying out in pain. Her plan to be beaten to death were thwarted by Listar, however. He stepped between Bel and Himeko.

"Until we receive payment in full, she is still my property, and I would rather keep her alive until our transaction is completed." Listar looked down his nose at the fat Tanis leader. Once he had control of the planet, he would work towards removing the privileged bastard. He hated working with a man he couldn't respect, but for now, Bel was a necessary evil.

Bel's body jiggled with contained rage. How dare this fur ball princeling stand in his way. Bel might not be able to physically oppose the Polaxian royal, but his mind was quick and devious. Already plans were forming to crush the Polaxians under the Tanis boot after Listar took control of a broken planet. The young prince never looked further than his desire for his father's throne to see what kind of peril his planet would be in.

Bel wanted to continue his assault on the twice-cursed Earth woman, but he could bide his time. The plague cure would be unloaded within the hour, then the little breeder would be his to do with as he pleased. After he finished with her it, would be just a few more weeks before the entire planet of Polax would be weakened to the point that conquering would be easy. Bel let Listar believe that the plague had been his own plan, but the Tanis had been maneuvering the Polaxians towards this for the last couple of years. They studied the royal family– played brother against brother until they found the prince that suited their purpose best.

Bel walked away with an evil smile on his face. Himeko knew that there was some plan working behind the scenes. Bel wouldn't put this much time and effort into a planet wide plan, even for revenge, if it didn't benefit him on a greater scale. Himeko shuffled through her history studies. She had found that many of the political strategies used between countries also worked on the grander scale between planets.

She remembered a lesson about the history of the Americas back on Earth. The United States army had distributed disease-infested blankets to the native population, causing an epidemic that weakened the people enough that the government could easily control the remaining population. Himeko shook her head. Listar was handing his people to Bel on a platter and he didn't even know it.

CHAPTER THIRTY-FOUR

Daray watched from the shadows as Listar exited his quarters. What he hadn't expected was to see Bel of the Tanis walking next to him. None of their observations or intelligence had said that Bel had returned to the planet. Daray knew that Bel was most likely the buyer, especially after Himeko had told him how she ended up fighting in the arena. Bel was a petty man, and he would trade vast amounts of credits, or in this case biological weapons, for the opportunity of revenge.

Daray cursed under his breath. He was fairly certain that Bel would leave Tanis guards to protect his investment. That would make getting to Himeko a little more difficult. Tanis soldiers had been trained on Vukas before the clan turned traitor. For that reason, the Tanis soldiers were more disciplined than the Polaxians.

Well, Raylan wanted a distraction. Daray would deliver one.

He took stock of what weapons he had with him. He carried two energy swords and a set of the old-fashioned bladed weapons for close combat. He was confident enough in his skills to know that he could win against half a dozen trained Vukasins, putting the odds in his favor. But fighting through a squad of men wouldn't get him and Himeko safely back to the rebel stronghold.

He could hear the words of Kavi during the special instruction for the future clan heads back when he, Reijo, and Ghaleb were still in their warrior's den. "Observe your surroundings. Adapt to the environment. Use what is at hand in unexpected ways."

Daray centered himself. The desperate concern for his mate was still there, but he pushed it from the forefront of his mind. He scanned the immediate area, taking note of every structure and person who passed by.

Four structures down, he saw a temporary

shelter that was quite a bit larger than the others. Unlike the others, the person stationed in front of it was a Polaxian female, not a male. Several males, both Tanis and Polaxian, stopped at the tent. The woman wouldn't let them enter until they had removed all of their weapons and placed them in a storage area near the door. Judging by the amount of weaponry piled inside, there was a large number of males inside.

Daray crept closer. The closer he got to the structure, the louder the sounds of sex and violence became. This was evidently the camp brothel, and Daray would lay a fortune in credits on the line that it was being manned by slaves who didn't have a choice about being there.

As much as his sense of justice wanted to rush in and free those women, Daray knew that he couldn't. Instead he would use the brothel as his distraction and pray that some of the women were able to escape in the confusion.

Daray only had his energy swords and the two metal blade weapons on his person. He briefly thought about trying to sneak into the armory tent to grab an explosive device, but that area was heavily guarded.

His mind shifted through several scenarios but they all came back to needing a fire or explosion to act as a distraction. Daray clenched his hands around the energy swords until his knuckles turned white. Then it clicked...an old memory from his childhood.

They had just been given their first energy swords and were learning how to use them. They had been instructed not to activate them unless an instructor was present. Of course, boys being boys, they rarely listened to their instructors and often broke the rules. He had been sparring with an older student in the woods behind the dormitories. The older boy was frustrated and angry that a much younger student had repeatedly bested him. In his anger, he had turned the energy sword up. It was no longer a blade that just delivered a sting when it touched skin, but now inflicted cuts. They fought some more and still Daray had out-skilled the older boy. After each bout, the older boy turned up the energy flowing through his sword, and even at lethal levels Daray still defeated him with his own blade set at practice levels. At the end, the older boy had turned up the energy as high as it would go, breaking the switch. This caused a feedback loop that eventually caused an explosion. It was powerful enough explosion that their instructors had come running and carted off the injured older boy. Daray never saw that boy again.

Shaking his head out of his memories, he looked down at the energy sword he held in his hand. If he could cause that feedback loop and plant the sword near the storage area housing the weapons of the men inside the brothel, he might be able to cause a cascade reaction that would result in a spectacular explosion. He could get Himeko out in the confusion and hopefully Raylan could get the cure.

Daray melted into the shadows and made his way to the brothel tent storage area. It was just a cloth tent. Daray shook his head. His men would never leave weapons unsecured like this in a war camp. But the Polaxian incompetence worked to his advantage. He pulled out one of his energy swords and tuned the blade of white pushing energy to their highest setting. When he heard the whine of the feedback loop, he lifted the back part of the storage tent and shoved the sword as deeply into the pile of weapons as he could manage. For good measure, he flicked on the energy of a few of the other swords piled in there. He remembered it took just a few minutes for the explosion to occur, so he quickly retreated towards Listar's quarters.

As Daray settled himself in the shadows of

Listar's temporary shelter the ground shook, and screams of men and women could be heard. A bright plume of fire filled the night air as smaller explosions could be heard going off in the night. Daray kept his eyes moving as Polaxians and Tanis soldiers rushed past him to help contain the flames. A few even rushed from inside Listar's shelter. Soon it seemed as if the area of camp that held Himeko hostage was nearly deserted.

Daray pulled his remaining energy sword from his belt and adjusted the blade to act as a cutting torch. He crept to the back of Listar's shelter and quickly cut a hole large enough to allow him entrance. He gingerly laid the metal skin of the shelter aside, ignoring the burn from the heated metal. He had to be as quiet as possible as he crawled into the shelter. When he raised his head, he saw his mate tied to a stake in the center of the shelter.

The two remaining guards were not paying attention to the battered woman. Instead they watched the brothel blaze from the doorway. When he crept over to his mate, he flinched when he saw the anger in her eyes instead of relief at her rescue.

Aho! Baka! I told you to get the cure. You are going to doom us all.

Daray reached over and caressed her cheek.

You are worth more to me than any number of worlds.

He could feel Himeko's heart melt at his declaration.

Daray....

I know the right thing would be to save the many at the cost of the few. But I was reminded by a friend that I didn't have to do everything alone...and neither do you.

A friend? Can you trust them?

Daray took one of the old-fashioned blades and cut through the bonds holding Himeko to the stake.

Raylan s using us as a distraction to get the cure. Can you stand?

I can't fight if I have to.

Daray pulled Himeko's war fan from his belt and placed it into her hands.

Good.

Daray had just pulled Himeko to her feet when one of the guards turned from the spectacle outside.

"Halt!" the guard cried as he lifted his pulse rifle. The second guard turned at his comrade's shout.

Himeko didn't hesitate. She ducked under the raised rifle and opened her *tessen*. She slashed the sharpened ends across the guard's throat. Blood exploded all over her. She turned on the second guard with unblinking eyes. Her war fan danced in front of her in hypnotic turns.

The guard backed away from the deadly tines until he ran into something warm and solid. His fatal mistake was overlooking Daray, who now held him. A swift swipe of the blade and the second guard was dispatched.

"We need to hurry before someone else comes to check on you." Daray grabbed Himeko's hand and dragged her out into the Polaxian camp.

Chaos still reigned as the fire had spread from the brothel to nearby tents. Daray used the disorder to melt back into the shadows with his mate. They moved quickly and quietly until they emerged from the Polaxian camp.

Daray breathed a sigh of relief thinking they had escaped unnoticed. He tugged on Himeko's arm as she stopped short suddenly. He wanted to get back to the stronghold quickly.

"Did you think to escape me so easily, breeder?"

Daray recognized the voice as Bel of the Tanis clan. A contingent of Tanis soldiers blocked the beach up ahead.

"I have to admit that the brothel was a brilliant distraction, and if my elite hadn't been here it might have succeeded. But we aren't so easily distracted as those Polaxian fools."

Daray and Himeko observed the group from the relative safety of a large boulder as Bel jerked his head until one of his soldiers dragged a beaten Raylan in front of them with another bound man who was the stature of a Ludian but didn't have their distinct coloring. He was blond and obviously ill.

"I think the other man is human," Himeko whispered to Daray.

"It wouldn't be surprising. I saw a few

human males up for auction. Evidently the Tanis are plundering your Earth for slave labor."

Their attention was brought back to Bel as he held up a large case and shook it in the air. "I just want you to know that you failed. The Polaxians will fall to our plague and even now we are sending the disease to Vukas. If the Vukasin people don't want to die, then they will bow their heads to their rightful masters…the Tanis!"

The end of Bel's speech was drowned out by the high-pitched whine of assault speeders swooping in from the darkened skies. Reijo had arrived. Weapons fired from the incoming speeders causing the Tanis to run for cover.

*****

"We have got to get the cure from Bel before he slip streams out of here!" Himeko was already running for the beach before Daray could stop her.

Himeko ignored the hands that attempted to grab her as she dashed towards Bel. She could feel Daray cursing impulsive women in her mind as he fought to catch up with her. Her smaller stature proved to be an asset as she made her way through the enemy.

She came face to face with the one man she felt was truly evil. Bel of Tanis didn't care who he hurt or killed as long as he got what he wanted in the end. She could see that the only reason the man hadn't escaped into the slip stream was because he wanted to cause Himeko as much suffering as possible.

She stopped a few yards short of the man who kept a blade at Raylan's throat. She shifted her eyes slightly to confirm that the body heat she felt at her back was Daray.

"The Nardo Princess," Bel spat. "You would be better named the Nardo whore!"

Himeko held up a hand when Daray would have charged Bel for those comments. This wasn't like Bel. Reijo's men were closing in and Bel was known for cutting his loses and escaping, but here he remained to taunt her and Daray.

Himeko just stared at Bel in silence waiting for his next move.

Bel suddenly jumped when one of the speeders fired near him. Raylan took that opportunity to wrench himself out of Bel's grip. Himeko was surprised when Raylan covered the weak and ill human with his own body as Reijo's men seemed to concentrate their attack on the area where Bel was. More likely than not, they recognized the man who had caused a lot of the chaos on Vukas.

Bel growled and dropped the blade he had in one hand and pulled a vial from the pack.

"At least I know you will die before I leave this accursed planet!" Bel bellowed as he hurled the vial at Himeko.

Time seemed to slow as the delicate glass container flew through the air. Raylan and the sick human both cried out when Bel released it towards Himeko. Daray shoved Himeko behind him. The vial shattered on his chest, covering him in what Himeko had to assume was the plague the Tanis had created.

Everywhere the contents touched skin, dark lines appeared in Daray's veins. Within seconds he had collapsed to his knees, his strength taken from him.

"No!" Himeko cried as she cradled her lover as he fell to the ground.

Her attention was drawn away from Daray at

Bel's roar of rage.

"Well, I won't get to watch you die like I hoped, but you and the Nardo fool are both doomed." He lifted the case that contained the plague vial and shook it at her with a sneer. "I'm the only one with the cure now." Bel gave an evil laugh.

Himeko heard the sound of several speeders landing near them as she gently laid Daray's head on the ground and stood. Bel heard them too as his eyes widened in a panic. The bastard started slapping at his chest as he backed up towards the water. Himeko knew that he was trying to find his personal slip-stream device. She had to get the cure before Bel was able to escape.

Bel finally hit the switch to activate his slip-stream device. Himeko could feel the air around them charging. It was impossible for her to cover the distance to get to Bel before he disappeared into the stream. She gripped her *tessen* in frustration. She really wanted to plant the war fan in Bel's throat.

The war fan…. It had been a long time since she attempted a throwing maneuver with the fan. In battle, it was impractical. The move was meant more for show. But just perhaps….

Himeko snapped her fan open. She gripped the last metal tine between her fingers, and with the fan wide open, she hurled it with all of her strength. The *tessen* whistled through the air as Bel started melting into the slip steam. Thank god that his massive bulk slowed the process somewhat.

To Himeko time stopped as she willed the war fan to hit its target. If her last ditch effort failed, then they were all going to die from the Tanis-created plague. She prayed to every deity she had ever learned of to let the fan land true.

Bel howled. Himeko's fan embedded in his forearm. The hand holding the case of vials opened with the impact and fell to the ground. Bel ripped the fan from his arm and disappeared into the slip stream with a percussive pop of air.

Reijo's men ran past Himeko in a futile effort to capture Bel of the Tanis. Himeko sunk down next to the now unconscious Daray. His breathing had become shallow. They needed to administer the cure to those who were the worst off and manufacture as much as they could in a short amount of time.

Reijo walked up behind Himeko and laid a hand on her shoulder. Himeko looked up at the *kijani-a* and sighed.

"Quarantine the planet, Reijo. Don't let any more soldiers on the surface. No one lands, no one leaves. Anyone already here is stuck here for a while."

"I'll have Megan contact Kavi. He will have to keep Ghaleb in line. Though can you tell me why?" Reijo knelt next to Himeko, taking the burden of Daray's limp body from her arms."

"The Tanis created a deadly plague. It affects basically every known species. They have already released it here on Polax, and from what I overheard I believe they plan to spread it to other worlds in a bid to take over the known galaxy."

"By the twin moons…I knew the Tanis were treacherous and ambitious…but that…that…."

"Falls into the realm of insanity." Himeko stood and walked towards the speeders with Reijo and her mate. "I think it is safe to say that Bel and his cronies view themselves more like gods than men." She turned back to the other Vukasin soldiers who were gathering Raylan and the injured human. "Make sure you bring the case and be careful. It carries both our doom and our salvation."

She turned back to Reijo after watching a

Vukasin soldier gingerly pick up the case.

"Do the rebels have anyone with the expertise to analyze and recreate the cure to this plague?" Reijo asked as he strapped the limp body of Daray to a speeder.

Himeko climbed up behind another officer and shook her head. "Honestly, I don't know. If not, you need to send a few Vukasin researchers down."

"That would put them in danger of contracting this plague themselves, M'lady!" the soldier transporting her gasped.

"We are all in danger of that anyway." Himeko gave an exhausted sigh.

"What do you mean by that?" Reijo demanded. He had Megan and their children to keep safe after all.

"I don't know if it is true or not, but Bel taunted us with the information that he had already sent carriers of the plague to Vukas. He plans on decimating the population until they beg the Tanis to take over in exchange for the cure."

The last thing Himeko heard was Reijo swearing as the speeder lifted off.

CHAPTER THIRTY-FIVE

Himeko watched helplessly as the medics administered another round of medication to Daray. It had been almost a week since Bel escaped after infecting Daray with the plague. They quickly discovered something that Himeko wasn't even sure the Tanis knew; the cure was simply a starting point.

The plague the Tanis created mutated rapidly. The cure was only truly effective as an inoculation against contracting the plague or a healing agent if administered right after exposure. After even a single day, the illness would be in its second generation and already mutating. Using what the Tanis thought of as the cure as a starting point had allowed them to slow the disease and, in a few cases, cure small numbers of the population. But it wasn't enough to lift the quarantine from the planet.

They needed someone whose expertise was in pathogens and how they spread and mutated. Unfortunately, major diseases had mostly been eradicated among the technologically advanced people of the various known planets. So few of the modern scientists and medics knew where to start, let alone how to get ahead of this manufactured disease.

They were making slow progress. Their treatments so far had slowed the killing, but thousands were still sick. Listar remained a threat even though, for now, he seemed content to wait until the disease decimated Alaric's forces.

Himeko moved to Daray's side as the medics left. He hadn't woken up since he was infected on the beach. Raylan and the human male, named John, both had mostly recovered from their exposure. Himeko, by some miracle, seemed to have a natural resistance, which allowed her to be inoculated before she contracted the disease.

The medics were making sure that Daray was given the fluids and nutrients he needed, but a week in a coma was beginning to show on her mate's body. Himeko was worried that even if they kept him alive, if they couldn't wake him up soon that he would just waste away before her eyes.

"Princess?"

Himeko didn't even look up from her mate when the voice called out to her. "I thought I told you not to call me that, Raylan."

The big Vukasin engineer who had appointed himself her protector sat next to her. She lifted her head and saw John hovering in the doorway.

"Since you brought John here, I doubt that this is a social visit. What did you want to tell me?" Himeko reached out and held Daray's hand. She really didn't care what was going on outside of this room, but she was still the diplomat for Vukas here. Reijo had taken over most of the duties that would have fallen to her since he was trapped here with the quarantine.

Raylan motioned John to come closer. The man was cute, even if he was rather timid. He made the picture-perfect academic, and Himeko briefly wondered where the Tanis had snatched him from.

"Um...the Vukasin medics won't give me access to the plague samples." John stated quietly.

Himeko gave an inelegant snort. "Of course

not. Even some of the medics aren't allowed near those samples. It's too dangerous to let just anyone near them."

"But I think I can help."

Himeko turned sharply towards John with narrowed eyes. "What do you mean?"

The man flinched slightly but stood his ground. "I'm an expert on deadly pathogens. I was a researcher for the National Center for Biotechnology under grants from the National Institute of Health."

Hope flared to life in Himeko's eyes. Then her mind started spinning through various scenarios. It wasn't coincidence that a human expert on deadly diseases was here. "This disease is human in origin, isn't it?"

John sat down. His whole body seemed to relax and take on a confidence he lacked before as the discussion turned to his area of expertise.

"There had been talk of *Y. Pestis* being genetically engineered to create a new terrorist weapon. Because of that chatter, my department had been tasked with researching various ways that the basic strain could be modified to be resistant to treatment and to come up with counter measures."

John seemed almost excited by the prospect of new diseases. It was a trait many scientists seemed to share. Science for science sake without thinking about possible consequences of what they were creating.

Himeko frowned, "*Y. Pestis?* The black death? Didn't that wipe out about three quarters of the European population at one time?"

John nodded. "Before the discovery of antibiotics, yes it did."

"So you are telling me that this disease is the black death? But I don't see the victims covered in bloody boils."

"I don't think the current disease can be classified as *Y. Pestis* any longer. But when the Tanis captured me and a few of my colleagues…." John's eyes clouded and he looked pensive.

Himeko laid a hand on his arm, "They died, didn't they?"

John blinked away tears. "We were used as the first test subjects. They didn't deserve that." John shook his head and looked Himeko in the eyes. "When they captured us they also took our samples that we were working on. I believe that this disease has a genetic ancestry in the black plague. That is my area of expertise. I'm also trained to combat outbreaks of deadly diseases."

Himeko thought for a moment. If what John was saying was true, he might just be the kind of expert they needed. Vukasin technology might be more advanced, but research is research and the Vukasins hadn't had to deal with an epidemic like this for generations.

Himeko stood and looked own at Daray. She really didn't want to leave him, but John might prove valuable.

Raylan saw her hesitate. "I'll stay with him, Princess. If anything changes you will be the first to know."

Himeko kissed her friend on the cheek. "Thank you." She turned to John and motioned for him to follow her. "I need to know everything you think you will need."

CHAPTER THIRTY-SIX

"Everyone is dying,"

Alaric leaned his forehead against the cool stone of the stronghold's window casing. He stared out towards the sea. Gone was the arrogant but naïve leader that Himeko had first met. In his place was a haggard man who feared for his people more than his position. It was a hard lesson but one that was well learned.

Alaric had seen what horrors blind ambition could wreck on his people with this plague Listar and the Tanis had released into the population. Alaric had held the hands of several people he had considered friends as they drew their last breath. He watched as parents went mad with grief after their child had died.

It had done more to make Alaric grow up to be the leader he needed to be than any lecture on politics and diplomacy that Himeko had ever given him. If they managed to survive this crisis, Alaric would be the exact person needed to help Polax rebuild.

"John and the Vukasin team are making progress. They discovered that there is a specific gene activated in those of us who seem to have a natural resistance...."

Himeko's explanation was cut short when an alarm sounded throughout the stronghold. Lack of personnel because of the plague and complacency since Listar hadn't attacked had left some of the areas undermanned. Evidently the royal Polaxian was just biding his time until he felt the rebels had weakened enough.

"Intruders...I repeat, intruders. The enemy has breached the stronghold. Last verified location: east wing, second level."

Himeko's heart nearly stopped; that was the hall that housed Daray's sick room. The man was slowly recovering since John had started working towards a cure, but he was still too weak to defend himself.

Alaric reached for Himeko, knowing she heard the same thing he had. Himeko shook off his grip and rushed out of the room, ignoring Alaric's calls for her to wait. She had waited and prayed while Daray fought off the cursed disease the Tanis had created. She had never felt so helpless waiting for fate to determine if the man she loved would live. Daray had finally broken through the illness and was weak but recovering. She would be damned if she allowed Listar to take him away from her now.

Himeko pulled her *tessen* from her belt and activated the special shield Dalir had created for the rebel's warriors. She had no doubt that Listar would be armed to the teeth this time. He was a spoiled, entitled piece of dragon-spider shit, but he was no fool.

Several of Reijo's men and a few rebels joined Himeko. They turned the corner to the corridor that had her and Daray's quarters in it, only to drop to the ground as the air filled with phase gun fire. Two of their men were hit and the rest cringed as they screamed until their bodies disappeared in a puff of ash, burned from the inside out. The fact that Listar's men were armed with phase guns instead of the pulse weapons let Himeko know that they were here to inflict as much lethal damage as possible.

Himeko and the others scrambled to get back to the relative safety of the corner.

"Who here has Dalir's new shield?" Himeko counted about a half dozen hands including herself. "Okay. Raise the shields to max power. We are going to act as the vanguard pushing the enemy back as the others prepare to attack behind us. Dalir said the shield should last for five direct hits at full power when it comes to the phase weapon. Keep count and get out of the way once you hit five, otherwise it won't be pretty."

All shuttered at the memory of the men they had just lost.

"Little bird….little bird, out of your cage."

Himeko closed her eyes and reached for the calm she needed in battle as Listar's mocking singsong voice echoed down the corridor.

"I have your mate, little bird." Listar chuckled. "Though why you chose such a weak creature is beyond me."

Himeko fought the urge to run towards Listar

and kill the man. She knew that his taunt was probably just a ruse to get her to expose herself.

"Himeko, *jinaria*, get far away from here."

Daray's weakened voice still held the strength of command. Himeko cursed silently to herself. Listar hadn't been lying. He had Daray. She knew that Daray was ready to sacrifice himself for her, but she refused to allow that.

Baka. Do you think I would just leave you to die?

I am too weak to be of any help to you, Himeko. The logical thing to do would be to get far away from here. I heard Listar talking; he wants you, Reijo, and Alaric. Everyone else is just target practice.

Himeko looked over her shoulder when she felt a hand placed there. She looked into the determined eyes of Alaric.

One way or another, this ends here, Daray.

Just live, my beautiful princess; because I will follow you wherever you go.

Himeko's heart and soul filled with the

warmth of Daray's love. He didn't try to demand she run away even though she could feel his desire for her to be away from danger and safe. He trusted her to make the best decision for both of them.

"Alaric, we don't have the time or resources to draw out a conflict with Listar." Himeko quietly explained to the rebel leader.

"I know, Himeko. This has to end here so we can concentrate on saving lives."

Himeko nodded. She quickly conferred with the men around her until they had a basic plan of action. She took one last peek around the corner to see Listar holding Daray like a shield in front of him. She would have to get up close and personal to kill the man without killing Daray in the process.

With a nod from Himeko, the vanguard activated their shields. They counted off and then burst around the corner as one unit. The rest of the people followed close behind.

Himeko gave a feral grin when she saw the panic in the eyes of Listar's men as they realized that their phase guns weren't having an effect on the people charging them. They were undisciplined bullies who had relied on greater fire power and brute strength instead of strategy.

Thankfully the charge made it to Listar's men before their shields gave out. The Vukasins and rebels crashed into Listar's men, disarming them as quickly as possible. The rebels to the rear of the group efficiently neutralized Listar's soldiers with blasts from their pulse guns. Most of the enemy would be incapacitated for several hours. A few fanatics had to be permenantly taken out.

Himeko was just a couple of yards away from Listar and Daray when the *frexing* ass ducked down a side corridor to try and make his escape. The man moved surprisingly fast for someone dragging an ill hostage with them.

Soon Himeko was separated from the rest of the fighting. She moved from the manmade corridors to the rough stone of the natural caves. She cursed her stupidity when she realized what had happened. She slowed down and proceeded with more caution. She wouldn't leave Daray to Listar's nonexistent mercies and it was too late to turn around to bring reinforcements.

"Little bird…little bird."

Listar's mocking voice echoed through the

caves. It was difficult to tell where the distorted sound was coming from. Himeko moved cautiously through the dark, concentrating on her connection with Daray. Listar had no way of knowing of her bond with the Nardo clan head. She ignored Listar's echoing voice. It was nothing but a distraction. She followed that mystical thread that seemed to bind her and Daray together.

Deeper and deeper into the caverns they went. The further away from the main stronghold, the darker it became as fewer light sources were lit to guide the way. If Himeko allowed herself to think of it, she would have panicked at the thought of having no way to find their way out once again even if she defeated Listar.

Himeko could feel Daray just up ahead. She felt his frustration at his weakened body and at her walking into danger to retrieve him. She gave a slight smile because, despite his thoughts on the matter, the man was smart enough to know that arguing with her would be a futile effort.

I still may spank your bottom for this madness when I recover.

Hmmm...that could have possibilities. Himeko flooded his mind with loving thoughts peppered with the occasional sensual image. She felt his amusement at her antics and eased some of the dread from his mind.

Himeko crept up to the area where she knew Listar and Daray had stopped. It was almost pitch black in the cave tunnels as the light sources were spaced far from each other, just enough light to indicate where another tunnel branched off. The darkness had worked in Himeko's favor, allowing her to creep within an arm's reach of Listar.

She planned a single killing blow. She raised her war fan to strike when the sound of someone bumbling over a stone behind her drew Listar's attention.

Listar whipped around, blinding Himeko with the lantern he had been using to navigate the dark corridors. She hissed and closed her eyes as she threw herself behind some rocks.

"Lady Himeko, are you down here?"

Colors still danced in front of Himeko's eyes as she cursed the idiots announcing their presence. She felt the air move before she heard Daray's warning in her mind. She rolled quickly and heard the clang of metal against the stone where her head had rested just a minute ago.

Memories of broken bones and her father's disappointment came to mind. The one item of training she had never been able to effectively master was a blind defense. She was going to die here because she couldn't master this technique and she would end up taking Daray with her.

Stop it now! Daray's firm voice filled her mind. She knew through their connection that Listar had tossed him aside to go after Himeko. His body was so weak from illness that he couldn't do more than drag himself to lean against one of the cavern stones.

We are stronger together, jinaria. Use our connection. See with my eyes if you have to.

Even with her eyes closed, the intrusive colors still flashed before her eyes. It was going to take a few minutes that she didn't have for her vision to clear. Tentatively she reached for Daray's whole mind instead of just the pieces he chose to share. She was swamped with emotion and memories. Part of her wanted to examine them, but she ruthlessly pushed them aside until all that remained was his vision.

Daray saw Listar raise his sword a second time as he moved around the bolder that Himeko had hid behind. Himeko caught sight of her own leg on the other side through Daray's eyes. She raised her war fan just in time to block Listar's blow. Himeko made a wild swipe with her *tessen,* causing Listar to back away with a smirk.

Himeko stood and moved into a fighting stance, only to have Listar laugh at her. It was difficult to discern which direction she should move because she was facing across from Daray, but seeing through his eyes wasn't like looking in a mirror.

Listar attacked. Himeko retreated as she felt the brush of a blade slicing the air beside her.

"Lady Himeko!"

Daray turned his gaze to the voice calling his mate, forcing Himeko to sever their connection or further disorient herself. But she saw Alaric and a group of rebels before she cut it off.

Daray! She growled in her mate's mind.

She tried her eyes once more as the colors had begun to fade. Her eyesight still wasn't at a hundred percent, but she could at least make out where Listar was.

"Little bird…little bird, let me clip your wings."

Himeko wondered if Listar had gone mad. "Finally lost your hold on reality, Listar? You know that the youngest son will never rule."

Listar gave a vicious laugh as he lunged at Himeko. "The rest are all dead. Once I get rid of great-uncle's by-blow, I will be the only royal left. Why do you think I allowed this plague to be released on Polax."

"You are a bigger fool than I thought," Himeko taunted as she attacked Listar. Slowly her vision was becoming clearer. She refused to stay on the defensive. "Even if you kill Alaric, you won't rule for long. The Tanis will swoop in and take over. The slavers will become slaves…. How ironic."

Listar howled in rage, which told Himeko that he had figured that much out for himself but was still hoping to get everything he wanted. He pressed his attack, forcing Himeko to retreat. Listar was as good a swordsman as any of the masters Himeko trained with in her youth.

"I will take the cure from you and the planet

will rally behind me!"

Himeko was about to inform him that there was no cure, just a base to work with, when her communicator went off.

"We are under a full-scale attack! Where the hell are you and Alaric?" Reijo demanded.

"Little busy," Himeko grunted. "We have problems of our own to deal with." She threw her communicator at Daray as she blocked and side stepped a thrust of Listar's sword. Thankfully, her eyes chose that moment to return to normal. *Thank the gods for small favors.*

Himeko could see Alaric positioning men at the various exits of the cavern. He then slowly started to creep up on Listar.

Himeko, Reijo says that the Polaxian forces are overwhelming the front lines because there aren't enough healthy people to man it.

Himeko cursed their luck. There was no way to defend this huge stronghold with so few people. They would have to somehow make the enemy too afraid to get close.

Tell Reijo to talk to Dalir. It's time to

release the shock and awe.

She could feel Daray's reluctance. She understood it. After all she grew up with the history of the atomic bomb being dropped on her people. But she knew they didn't have a choice. This wasn't about the succession of power on a single planet any longer. They had a potential galaxy-wide deadly epidemic in the making. They had to retain control of the only samples that could lead to a cure.

Her thoughts had strayed too far from the battle she was fighting. Her distraction allowed Listar to get under her defenses. Himeko felt the burning cut as her enemy's blade sank into her side. She knew from that angle he most likely hit her kidney. It was a killing blow and she knew it as she sank to the ground even as Daray screamed his denial in her mind.

CHAPTER THIRTY-SEVEN

Daray watched as the woman he loved collapsed to the ground, her life blood spreading out around her. He tried to stand to rush to her, but his legs were still so weak that they wouldn't support him. He used his hands and called on every ounce of strength and a few prayers to the gods to crawl towards her prone body.

Listar raised his sword to finish the job and Daray roared his rage. Suddenly, Listar's body jerked and his eyes rolled back into his head. His sword fell from limp fingers as he slowly fell across the injured Himeko. Alaric stood behind the man with a raised pulse rifle. By the look on his face, Daray knew that was the first time Alaric had fired on a live person.

Daray pulled himself next to Himeko and tried to push the dead weight of Listar off of her. Once again he cursed his weakened state. Alaric, carrying his rifle, came and helped him move Listar's body. And it was a body. Daray could see the sightless stare of the man who was the cause of all of this madness. He sighed, not because of the loss of a madman but because he knew that Listar's face would haunt Alaric as his first kill.

Daray turned his attention back to Himeko, whose breathing was becoming labored and shallow. She reached out and touched his face.

"I will always love you," she gasped.

Daray entwined his fingers with hers and felt her body go limp as she lost consciousness.

"No, no…No! You can't leave me!" Daray had tears flowing down his cheek. "I promised that I would follow wherever you go. So stay here with me."

Daray patted her cheek but couldn't rouse her. Despite him holding a hand over the wound in her side, her blood still flowed too fast from her. He desperately looked around but only saw the rebels.

"I need a Vukasin soldier." Daray's bloody

hand clutched at Alaric. For a moment Alaric had thought that Daray had gone mad with grief since it was clear that Himeko was dying. But the earnest look in the Nardo clan head's eyes pushed Alaric to find him what he asked for.

Thankfully a contingent of Vukasin soldiers were already heading towards the cavern. When Alaric informed them that Himeko was mortally injured, one soldier broke away and took off at a dead run to get to her and Daray.

Daray stared at Himeko's chest as if sheer will could keep her alive. He barely flicked his eyes towards the soldier who slid to a halt next to him. Quickly he pulled a portable regen unit out and slapped it on Himeko's stab wound. She didn't even flinch at the forceful treatment.

The bleeding started to slow and Daray finally looked up. He recognized the young man who was currently trying to stabilize his mate. He was Reijo's cousin, if he remembered correctly. If memory served, he was a well-respected medic.

"You're Elod, aren't you?"

The young man didn't even look up from his tasks. "Yes, I am. Himeko is one of my friends through Megan. Now let me work."

Daray was actually encouraged by the man's abrupt, no nonsense demeanor. He knew that Himeko had his full attention. As the man worked, a crowd of rebels and Vukasins alike gathered around the fallen woman. Someone had removed the body of Listar to make room.

The bleeding finally stopped, but Himeko's breathing remained shallow and she was so pale from blood loss that she almost looked dead. Elod straightened with a heavy sigh.

"The portable unit was able to temporarily seal the cut vessels. Her kidney has been badly damaged and she needs surgery. It is even possible that she will have to have that organ removed. Thankfully, humans have two kidneys and can survive without one, though we could grow a replacement in a lab if necessary. We need to get her aboard ship so I can get her into surgery. I can't do that here." Elod spoke into his communicator. "I need a stasis unit down here immediately and arrange transport to the ship." Elod frowned at the response he was receiving, "I don't care about the quarantine. Himeko has been disease free this entire time…. Fine, you can explain to Reijo and Megan why one of their best friends died because of *frexing* paperwork…. I thought you would see it my way, now get moving."

Elod switched off the communicator and Daray smiled at the man. "You would make a pretty good general."

Elod made a face and Daray chuckled. The pair said nothing but continued to watch Himeko breathe. Alaric was finally acting like the leader he needed to be, directing the others to sweep for more enemies and secure the area. Maybe this whole ordeal matured him.

It seemed like hours, even though Daray knew that it was only minutes, before a team of medics arrived with the stasis unit and anti-grav sled to transport Himeko. A pair of medics helped Daray to his feet and steadied him while the others gently moved Himeko to the sled.

Elod turned to Daray and the medics supporting him, "You need to go back to your quarters and get some rest. This incident may have pushed your recovery back a few days."

"I'm going with you." Daray frowned. They had to know that he wouldn't allow himself to be parted from Himeko.

Elod shook his head. "You are barely recovering from the plague and we still aren't certain of how easily it is transmitted to others. Bringing Himeko off planet is a risk, but a measured one since she has been inoculated and she had a natural resistance anyway. Even so, I am quarantining one operating room and regen unit. We will be slip-streamed directly to those areas after a forcefield is erected and we won't leave those areas before returning to the surface. You, on the other hand, are a risk I cannot take."

"But—"

Elod held up a hand to stop Daray, "I know your feelings, but use that logic and fairness you are so famous for. Would you risk the whole ship for your selfishness? Hundreds of lives because you want your eyes on your mate?" Elod laid a hand on Daray's shoulder, "You can't help and would be more in the way. Stay here, recover so you can be there for her when she needs you to be."

"Has anyone told you that you are a pain in the ass when you are right?" Daray conceded.

"Reijo says the same thing all of the time." Elod laughed as he and the medic team slowly started moving Himeko towards the stronghold.

Reijo had put up a temporary slip-stream device in the main hall.

Daray sighed but allowed the medics supporting him to take him to his quarters.

CHAPTER THIRTY-EIGHT

"It's been almost a month, Raylan, and I haven't seen my mate," Daray groused.

Raylan popped a piece of fruit into his mouth and chuckled. "You knew that as soon as she found out about the deaths of the rest of the royal family she would be busy."

Daray flopped down on the cushioned couch. He had to admit that quarantine was much more comfortable now that they had moved to one of the royal palaces. "Of course, I knew she would be busy, but I also expected to at least be sharing quarters with her." Daray sighed. "Hell even you have time to chase after John."

Raylan choked on the piece of fruit he had just popped into his mouth and had to beat his chest to try and dislodge it. While his eyes teared as his airway cleared, he was glad to see a smile ghost across Daray's face. The man had been downright morose ever since they took Himeko away for surgery.

"How...how did you know?" coughed Raylan.

"Honestly," Daray had a wistful look as he stared out the window into the bright sky, "I didn't. You were always just Raylan. I chalked the fact that you didn't show interest in women to the fact that even now with the women from Earth and Ludus Prime, there are few women available to Vukasin men." He turned back to his childhood friend with a slight smile. "After we tried to beat the crap out of each other, Himeko told me why I was such an idiot to be so jealous of you. And after you found John being experimented on, it wasn't that hard to see that you had a similar look in your eyes when you look at him as I do when I look at Himeko."

Raylan looked down and his shoulders slumped slightly. "Yeah I can look all I want, but that doesn't mean anything. Especially since the quarantine will be lifted soon and we will be leaving."

"That's right. John is going to stay here and head up the interplanetary center for disease control. Even if we beat this plague, there is always the possibility of another one sometime in the future."

"And you are going to stay here and help."

Both men jumped to their feet at the sound of a familiar feminine voice. Daray rushed over and crushed her in an embrace until she had to hit his arm to loosen his grip so she could breathe. She gave her mate a loving kiss and leaned against him as she turned her attention back to their friend.

"They need good engineers and I put your name in to head that department. The Kassians and Ludus Prime are sending scientists and engineers to work at the new center as well. The royal council wants people we can trust working this project. This has both the potential to greatly benefit the known galaxy or be a source of its demise. We need people we know will hold the good of the populace as their primary motivation."

"I can stay here." Raylan sunk down into his seat in shock.

"Yes, you can," Himeko smiled as she moved

to give her friend a hug. "Time to use that charm of yours to find happiness."

Daray wrapped his arms around her waist and pulled Himeko towards the door.

"Where are we going?" she asked.

"To find our own happiness, *jinaria.*"

EPILOGUE

"I can't do this."

Himeko paced nervously in the room reserved for her at the temple complex by the sea. The temple grounds were filled to overflowing with members of the Nardo clan and dignitaries from several other planets.

Daray snuck in to see the bride, against tradition, only to find her panicking.

"You have spoken before entire planetary governments. You will be fine." He wrapped his arms around her and gave a comforting squeeze.

"That crowd is expecting some beautiful mythical princess...I can't live up to that expectation." Himeko turned to Daray and laid her hands on his chest. "Let's run away...we are already mated by Vukasin standards; we don't have to do this."

Daray kissed her forehead so he didn't mess up her elaborate make-up and hair. She had decided to dress in traditional formal attire of her heritage. It was quite different from the long white gown that Megan had decided on for her ceremony with Reijo, even if it was also white in color.

Daray studied his beloved mate. Her pale make-up with the delicate red lips, together with the elaborate hair style with jeweled pins sparkling already made her look like something out of a story. The kimono, as he learned, hid the delicate curves of her body but somehow made her appear elegant and refined.

"You are already their princess, Himeko. All you have to do is walk out and let them see how beautiful you look and the entire planet will be jealous that I claimed you as my mate first."

She smiled up at the handsome man who was the love of her life and about to be her husband. He was particularly handsome today in his ceremonial uniform as the Nardo clan head. Suddenly she shoved him out of the door.

"Go. If you are at the end of the aisle, then I will make it." She gave him a brilliant smile. "All I have to do is keep my eyes on you."

Daray leaned down and kissed her forehead. "I will follow you anywhere, *jinaria,* even unto the next world."

With his vow, he turned to go wait for his bride in the temple. Himeko blinked back tears. She was finally where she belonged.

ABOUT THE AUTHOR

B.D. Snowden is a Texas native living in the Great Plains with her children of both two-legged and four-legged varieties. She is a voracious reader whose book habit literally brought a small town library to life. One day, when she was unable to get something new to read, she started turning the stories floating through her head into concrete concepts on paper.
Find information about new releases and appearances at:
Geekygothblog.wordpress.com
Facebook.com/BrandiceSnowdenWriter

www.ingramcontent.com/pod-product-compliance
Lightning Source LLC
Chambersburg PA
CBHW061310170626
46817CB00001B/129